MY SWEET VALENTINE

THE PRIDE SERIES

JILL SANDERS

GRAYTON

To my greatest love and best friend, My Husband

SUMMARY

Sara Lander was back in town. She had big plans for her inheritance along with her freshly printed business degree and years of experience in some of Seattle's finest bakeries. She also had a rich idea for Pride. Sara's Nook was going to be the next biggest thing to hit town. All she needed now was to steer clear of the hunky ex-Navy SEAL who was hell-bent on taking all her focus away from starting her own business.

Allen Masters had been living in Pride for several years. Setting up a new branch of the Coast Guard and training all the new recruits took years of skill and all his patience. But when he saw the black-haired beauty who had come back into town, he realized she was the one he'd been searching for. Taking one taste of her sweets, he knew he'd be in for a sinful time, but losing his focus while flying into the eye of a storm was the last thing he could afford.

PROLOGUE

*A*llen struggled to hold the Blackhawk steady. He could hear the bullets flying by and, for just a second, he closed his eyes and prayed. Then he took a deep breath and pointed the nose of the chopper where he needed to be. Signaling his crew, they were in position, he held his hands steady as his men extracted the Marines from the site.

All his concentration was on keeping the bird steady. His crew was working on the last Marine when he felt the sting in his chest. The bird jolted to the side as debris from the tempered glass flew around his face, hitting his helmet and knocking off his face shield. Warning sirens went off, signaling that the chopper was in trouble. His crew screamed in his ear as he gripped the stick with both hands, which was slick with his own blood. His vision threatened to fade, so he bit the inside of his cheek and held on. Looking behind him, he saw that the last Marine was safe, so he pointed the bird into open skies.

"Allen!" his co-pilot Mayer yelled at him in the head-set. "You got this?"

"Yeah. I got this." The sound of gunfire faded away as they hit open sky. His chest was on fire and breathing was getting difficult. He felt the chopper tilt and heard a new group of alarms going off. This time he knew there was no way to pull the bird up from the nosedive.

Yelling to the back for everyone to hold on, he relayed his location information to the base as they spiraled out of control towards the desert floor.

A second before impact, his mind flashed to a peaceful image of him sitting on a beach somewhere, a large, hairy black dog running in the surf after a stick, a woman's gentle hand touching his arm. The second he turned to look at her, the bird hit the desert floor. Pain exploded in his body until all he knew was darkness.

When he surfaced again, it was to his crew screaming his name. Private Steven's was standing over him, yelling for him to get out. Then the next minute, the man was dead, hunched over the console, half his face gone from a round. The shock tried to force Allen to freeze up, but he'd been trained for this. Since his body was sheltered from the incoming rounds, he stayed down. Looking behind him, he could see the other men in his team looking at him for instructions.

"Stay down. Stay put until we see where it's coming from," he said into his headset.

"The ridge on the left. We've tried to get the shooter, but he's in there tight." Lt. Miller, their sharpshooter, sounded pissed. "He picked off two of the Marines before we could get behind cover."

"Damn." His team had risked their lives for those

Marines and to have two of them gone while he was out, just pissed him off. "Is there only the one shooter?"

"Yeah, we landed in a pretty remote area. Base says Humvees are en route."

"Miller do whatever it takes to take him out. I'll cause a distraction. When he pops his head up, take him out."

Allen reached around and unbuckled himself. Slowly he slid to the left and out of the seat. He could see the desert floor jutting up into his view. In the distance, he saw a flash a second before Miller's shot rang out. The hidden sniper's bullet grazed his helmet as Miller's round took him down.

"Better stay down, just in case there's more." Allen looked around the desert hills and after a few minutes of silence, everyone relaxed and waited for the convoy to come to pick them up.

Allen sat there quietly waiting for rescue, bleeding through a hole in his side, dreaming of a beach, a dog, and a woman.

CHAPTER 1

ive years later…

Allen was caged in again. Every time he turned to get away, there was another opponent. They were faster, smaller, and younger than he was. Even though they were well matched in numbers, his crew was about to get their butts whipped. He went in for a kill, only to get stuffed and served.

"Get behind him, let's try that one again," Aaron, his captain, said as they huddled together. "We've got these twerps. We aren't going to let a bunch of greasy-faced teenagers take us down, are we?"

"It's now or never." Allen knew they had to gain the higher ground again. He looked around, trying to avoid the watchful eyes, knowing the distraction could end up killing them.

"Break." They parted ways as the buzzer sounded the timeout was over.

When the ball was in motion again, he realized there was no way they were going to win. Those greasy kids were going to whip their butts. They made three more points to the teenagers' five before there was a squeal, causing the entire gym to look towards the bleachers.

"Aaron, your wife's water just broke. You better get over here and take her in. You're having a baby," said Megan Jordan. She stood by the petite Lacey Stevens, who was past her due date and stood there holding her protruding belly. Aaron, along with Lacey's two brothers, Iian and Todd, rushed off the court and lifted her down gently from the bleachers. Luke and Allen stood there trying to catch their breath. They smiled and watched their friends all hover as Aaron carried his wife out the doors. Several of the women who'd been cheering them on left.

Two women remained. They talked as the other team and the referee left.

"Is that Amber, the new manager for the Golden Oar?" Allen slapped Luke's back as he looked at the pretty brunette. He kept trying not to look at the raven-haired beauty standing next to Luke's new girl.

"Yeah." Luke smiled in her direction. Allen knew Luke and Amber had been seeing each other for about a month. Luke's grandmother had died recently, and he'd been going through a rough time. But seeing Luke's smile and watching his eyes light up when he looked at Amber, he knew he'd gotten through the hardest part.

The black-haired beauty standing next to Amber had been introduced to Allen before the game as Sara Lander, an old friend of Allison Jordan's. Sara had been born and raised in Pride, but for the past three years had been living in Seattle. He didn't know much more, but curiosity was killing him.

Luke waved to Amber and started to walk towards the locker rooms. Allen followed him, trying to keep his eyes from traveling to the two women standing by the bleachers. He couldn't understand why he was feeling a pull towards Sara, but he was, and he was the last person to deny an instinct.

"So, you grew up here?" Allen asked while the two men showered in separate stalls.

"Yeah, I moved east after school and spent some time at MIT." There was a moment of silence. "Why?"

"Well, I figured you could fill me in on what you know about Sara." He tried to sound casual, but his friend easily caught on and for the entire time they were in the showers and getting dressed, Luke gave him shit over it. He did get some useful information from his friend, but Luke spent most of the time getting back at Allen for all the shit he'd given Luke over the last few weeks about his feelings towards Amber.

With the tables turned, Allen knew he was in for it. He just smiled and returned the humor when he could.

When they walked out to the gym, Allen was a little disappointed to see Amber standing there alone, waiting for Luke. He watched the couple leave and felt a twinge in his chest. Why did it feel like he'd found everything he'd been dreaming of that fateful day when his chopper had gone down except the one thing he desired most?

He walked out, then hopped in his truck and checked his messages while his truck warmed up in the parking lot. He enjoyed his job as company commander of the new

Coast Guard base. When he'd arrived that first day to check out the facility, he'd walked out on the beach and sat on a large piece of driftwood. He'd known instantly that he'd found the right spot. It had taken him several months to tie up loose ends and find a place to live. He'd been lucky to find an older house just on the outskirts of town that needed a little work. It had been easy enough fixing the house up. The new headquarters for the Pride Coast Guard was a different story; it had taken almost a year to turn the old sawmill into the top-notch facility it now was.

Over a thousand recruits had come in and out of the front doors of that place last year. So many that they'd turned one of the outbuildings into barracks to house all the recruits. Now, less than a year later, they were building another, larger building to the south of the original facility to house even more recruits. They were also adding a large kitchen facility along with a medical center. The small town of Pride was growing bigger thanks to the Coast Guard, and Allen was in charge of it all.

There were those in town who didn't want over two hundred recruits running around town, but for the most part, people seem to appreciate the change and the added notoriety that came with having the Coast Guard at their doorstep.

Even though the facility only housed the school, they had an active branch that could, at a moment's notice, whisk away to be out on a call. Allen had gone on a dozen or so calls in the last year alone. Most of them were fishing boats that needed help. Some were recreational vehicles that had gotten themselves in trouble. But, to date, Allen had not felt the stress and pressure that he had overseas.

Allen drove off through town and noticed someone

standing out in the rain on Main Street. When he looked closer, he realized it was Sara. He quickly pulled over, his first thought being that her car had broken down. But when he pulled up, she turned from looking into an empty building and waved at him.

Sara stood on the sidewalk in front of the large building, looking into the windows. The empty building was dark, but if she cupped her hands, she could see all the way to the back of the empty room. It was huge. Bigger than she needed. Her heart skipped a few beats as she mentally designed the space.

She heard a car drive up and turned and watched Luke get out of his truck and open the door for Amber. Sara had just met Amber a half-hour ago at the gym while they watched the men playing basketball. Apparently, she was the new manager at the Golden Oar.

Sara had been visiting Allison to see her and Iian's son, Conner. Allison was one of her closest school friends. When she'd gotten there, Allison had invited her to go watch the guys play a game against some teenagers at the Boys and Girls Club.

"Hi." Sara waved to them and walked across the street. Luke looked at her like she was crazy for standing out in the cold, and she explained, "I was just driving by and saw the 'for sale' sign and thought I'd stop and look."

"Are you in the market for an old building?" Luke asked.

She laughed. "Yes actually, I've been thinking about opening a bakery." Sara turned back towards the building.

"It's a lot bigger than I'd planned, but I think it'll work." She turned back towards them. "I could even have tables in the front and offer breakfast items. The Golden Oar is great, but they don't open until lunch. I could sell coffee, donuts, and muffins. Not to mention cakes and pies."

Luke took Sara's hand in his. "Marry me." He laughed, and she could see the humor in her old friend's eyes. He'd always been a joker.

"Luke, you know I'd never marry you." She laughed and punched him on the arm. "Do you know if Allison's family still owns the building?" She'd never thought to ask Allison before. She knew her friend was probably busy at the hospital with Lacey and their family.

"I think so, but you might want to ask next time you see her. I expect a party the second that baby arrives. Maybe this time tomorrow?" Luke took Amber's hand and Sara realized she was probably holding them up.

"Yeah." Sara bit her lip and turned back towards the building. "Maybe I will ask her." She turned back towards them and said, "I didn't mean to interrupt your plans. Have a great night." She turned and walked back across the street.

She felt a little sad as she watched her friend walk up the stairs on the side of the local mart. She knew there was a large apartment Patty O'Neil rented out. When the lights turned on in the apartment, she turned and walked back to the empty store and realized she could now see into the empty building even better.

Leaning her face against the cold glass, she didn't hear the second car approach until it passed her and stopped on the wrong side of the street right next to her.

"Did your car break down?" His voice was deep and

instantly she felt the warmth spread up her spine. Turning, she looked up. It was dark inside his truck, but she could make out his profile. She'd seen him for the first-time half an hour ago and she still felt the shock from that first view. Taking a deep breath, she walked over to his truck and placed her friendliest smile on her face.

"No, just looking at an empty building. Thanks for stopping though." She hoped he'd drive away soon. Being this close to him was doing something to her. She was actually shaking.

"Can't you look at it in the daylight when it's not this cold out?" His voice was laced with concern.

She smiled again. "I guess I'm used to the cold." She tucked her hands into her heavy coat pockets. Her gloves were keeping them warm enough, but she was beginning to feel the chill. "I can't really see anything tonight anyway. Thanks for stopping and checking on me."

She could see him frown. "Why are you looking at an old building?" He looked behind her at the empty spot.

If she kept telling people, no doubt the news of her business venture would be all over Pride before she got a chance to talk to Allison about the space. "It used to belong to Allison. I'm just checking up on it."

He frowned again and looked down at her. There was an awkward moment of silence. "Well, I'll wait until you get in your car."

She huffed out her breath. He really wasn't going to leave until she got in her car. She felt like he was babysitting her. She was an adult. She could take care of herself. Pulling her shoulders back, she turned and walked to her car and got in. His truck lights blinded her as he sat behind her car. It was after six in the evening in Pride, and everyone was having dinner, tucked nice and warm in their homes.

She pulled her keys from her coat and turned them only to have her car sputter as she tried to start it. She'd just gotten a tune-up before she'd left Seattle. She punched the gas pedal a few times with her foot and tried again. She could feel the lights from Allen's trucks boring into her back.

"Come on! Start. Don't embarrass me in front of him." She tried again, only to have her car completely stop making any noise. "No, no, no. Don't do this. Please." When she tried again, she realized it wasn't going to happen.

She jumped when he knocked on her window. He stood outside, his coat and hat sheltering him from the light snow that had just started. She leaned over and rolled down her window.

"Won't start?" He leaned closer.

"No." She looked down at her car gauge. The engine light was on.

"Might need a new battery. If you want, I can take you home and you can deal with it in the morning."

She looked straight ahead and felt the shaking starting again. "No, that's okay. I live just a few—"

"Lady, I wouldn't let my worst enemy walk a block in this weather. Gather your stuff up, I'll drive you wherever you need to go." He opened her door and stood back, waiting for her to get her things.

Again, she felt like she was left no choice. She knew he was the commander at the Coast Guard, so he was probably used to getting his way. That didn't mean he could boss her around. She gathered up her purse and decided everything else in the car could wait until the morning.

When she got out, she realized how tall he was. She had to look up to him when she spoke. "It's very nice of you to offer, but I'll be just fine. I only live two blocks away."

"I'm just trying to be neighborly. I'm Allen Masters, by the way. We weren't formally introduced." He stood there and smiled at her. She felt a little of her resolve melt; he had a great smile.

"Yes, I know. I'm Sara Lander. It's nice to meet you."

During the basketball game, Allison had told her all about Allen. How he'd come into town and taken charge of all the construction, turning the old mill into the newly renovated facility the Coast Guard now used. Apparently, he was also a pilot and went out on rescues all the time. Surely, she could trust someone who risked his life every day to save others.

"Well." She looked up at him and realized how good looking he was. Too much man, she thought. She felt like a teenager standing next to Tom Selleck in his heyday. What would she do with a man like him? She'd only dated one person seriously before and he didn't look like this. Allen was probably in his early thirties. His dark hair was covered with a ball cap with a Coast Guard patch. His brown leather coat looked loved and worn in places. His jeans were the same, faded and worn out.

According to Allison, he'd been overseas in the war. She probably had nothing in common with him. He most likely found her to be irritating. Especially since she'd kept him standing on the sidewalk for a few minutes now.

Pulling her bag close to her, she nodded her head and

raised her chin. "Fine. You can drive me home." She started walking towards his truck and thought she heard him laugh. "Did you say something?" She turned and looked at him, her eyebrows raised in question.

He smiled. "No, ma'am." He rushed to the passenger side of his truck and opened the door for her. She stood there looking at the large truck, trying to figure out how to get in it.

"If you grab onto that handhold there, you can step on the running board and pull yourself in." He smiled.

She did as he suggested. It took her two tries to pull herself into the large vehicle. As he walked around the front of the truck, the heat hit her full force and she realized she was freezing. Her teeth started chattering the second he opened his door. She clenched her jaw to keep from letting him know how cold she was.

"I'm sorry, I guess I didn't realize how tall my truck is." He smiled at her and she could tell he was trying to hold back laughter.

She nodded her head, not wanting to open her jaw in case her teeth should start banging together. He pulled into Main Street and started driving up the hill slowly. "Where to?" He looked over at her.

"Two blocks up, one to the right." The warmth inside the cab was quickly heating her. When he looked at her, she felt heat spreading from her insides as well.

"So, are you going to tell me why you were really looking at the empty building?"

She quickly looked at him, trying to figure out how he knew she'd lied to him. When he just continued to smile, she told him.

"I'm thinking of opening a bakery. Well, I've been

thinking of it ever since I saw the empty building." She looked out the window. He was driving too slowly for her liking.

"Bakery, huh?" She turned and saw him looking straight ahead, thinking. "Are you any good at baking?"

"It does help to be good at it, in order to run my own bakery." She laughed.

"I like that." He smiled at her and she felt her stomach flutter.

"What?" She tried not to notice how nice his smile was. "That I can bake?"

"No, your laugh." He glanced at her again. "You should do that often."

She frowned a little. She didn't know what she should do now. Thank him? She was saved when he continued on.

"What kind of things would you sell in your bakery? Cakes? Brownies?"

"Yes, a little of everything. The nearest bakery is in Edgeview. They do a lot of cake orders for birthdays, weddings, and everything. But I was also thinking of doing sandwiches. Cold and hot."

"Do you know how to make bagels?" He shook his head. "I haven't had a good bagel since Boston."

She laughed. "Yes, actually, they are one of my favorites as well."

He looked over at her and smiled. "I'd do just about anything for a loaded bagel with whipped strawberry cream cheese on top."

She imagined exactly what she'd like him to do, causing her cheeks to heat. "There, it's the last house on the left." She turned her face away, hoping he hadn't noticed them turn bright red.

He pulled into the drive and quickly got out. Before she could gather her bag, he was opening her door and holding his hand out for her to take.

She put her gloved hand in his while trying to step down on the running board but ended up falling forward straight into his arms. His muscled arms wrapped around her and she felt how solid his chest was against her own. He smelled of shampoo and leather, a wonderful combination. She looked up and started to apologize, her face so close to his she could feel his breath on her face.

"I'm—" Then his lips were on hers and she forgot where she was and what was happening. He tasted like heaven and just the feel of his warm mouth on hers sent every remaining chill from her entire body. Not only did she forget to breathe, she forgot to move and stood encased in his arms like a statue as his mouth moved over hers.

He pulled back and smiled down at her. "Sorry, I must have slipped."

She would have laughed if she'd regained any of her senses, but instead, she just nodded her head and lowered her eyes to the V of his jacket.

What did someone do with someone like him? A more sophisticated woman would have laughed and flirted with him. But she was having a hard-enough time putting two words together to make a sentence.

Just then the front porch light went on and she pulled out of his arms, almost slipping on the ice in her driveway.

"My mother." She didn't know why she'd felt the need to explain things to him, but he smiled and dropped his arms.

"Well, if you can't get the car started in the morning,

give Rusty a call. He'll fix it up for you real fast." He shoved his hands into his pockets.

She hoisted her bag over her shoulder. Everyone from Pride knew about Rusty, the only mechanic in a thirty-mile radius. Sara didn't know what to say, so she just nodded and started walking towards the front porch, then stopped and turned around.

"Thanks for the ride." She didn't want to seem rude. Her mind had just clicked into gear and she realized she was about to walk away without thanking him.

He nodded and smiled. "Anytime." He turned and got back into his truck, waiting in the driveway until she was safely inside.

When she closed the door, Becca, her sixteen-year-old sister jumped on her. "Who was that?" She sat on the edge of the couch and peered out the front blinds.

"Allen Masters. My car wouldn't start, and he stopped and offered me a ride." She tossed her bag onto the couch and walked into the kitchen to find her mother sitting at her desk in the corner, working on her computer. Her mother looked more like Becca than Sara. They had the same build, tall and skinny. Her mother's short gray hair looked stylish and her silver earrings bobbed up and down. Her mother was a chain smoker but had recently quit. Now she chose to compensate by chewing on Nicotine gum all the time. "Evening, Mom. What would you like for dinner?"

It had been the same every night for the last several weeks since she'd gotten home. If Sara didn't cook dinner, Becca and their mother would eat something microwaved that had more chemicals in it than the boxes the food was packaged in.

Even though she loved her family, she was ready to find a place of her own. Becca had been allowed to run wild since Sara had left several years ago. It wasn't Becca's fault, really. Their mother had spoiled her from the moment she'd been born. Sara, on the other hand, had taken over the parent role since the fifth grade, when their father had packed his bags and moved to Vegas with their mother's best friend. Neither Becca nor Sara had seen him since.

"Whatever you want, dear. I can always heat something up."

"No." Becca jumped in, walking over to the countertop. "Sara doesn't mind cooking, do you?" Her sister was a lot taller than Sara's own five-foot-five frame. Not to mention she had more curves than her and her hair was lighter than her own. Basically, Becca was the pretty child. Sara had curly, raven hair, but she'd never really looked at it as beautiful, just a nuisance to take care off. Mostly, she kept it tied back out of the way as she baked. Tying it back now, she got to work making spaghetti for her family as she thought of Allen Masters and the kiss that had baked her insides.

CHAPTER 2

A few days later, Allen bumped into Sara at Aaron and Lacey's house. Everyone in town was there to celebrate the arrival of their son, George. He'd been hoping he'd bump into her again. He didn't know what had come over him in her driveway, but he couldn't deny what the kiss had done to his system. He'd thought of little else since then and knew he wanted to kiss her again.

She was wearing tight red pants with a large black sweater hanging over her hips. Her hair was tied up in a roll with curly wisps falling all around her face. He'd noticed her eyes, how dark brown and beautiful they were, the first time he'd seen her. But the way her lips tasted like strawberries, and the way they felt like silk, had sealed his interest in her. Her body had been soft next to his and somehow fit perfectly against his own.

When he walked across the room and came up to her, he could see her cheeks turn a little pink and a slight fear come into her eyes.

"Hello." He smiled when she almost dropped the plate

of food she'd been holding. "Easy." He reached over and took her hand under the paper plate to steady her.

"Hi...hello." She looked around the room quickly, making it appear as if she was looking for a way to escape. Why did he get the idea she was afraid of him? He'd just have to show her he was an all-around good guy.

"Here." He motioned towards a small couch that had been abandoned. "Why don't we sit so you can finish that?" He took her elbow and steered her toward the darkened corner.

When they sat, he made sure to give her plenty of room. She looked down at the food and he could tell she had lost all interest in finishing the plate.

"How's the bakery idea going? Have you had a chance to talk to Allison yet?" He watched as she leaned over and set the plate on the small table next to the couch.

"Oh!" Her face lit up. "Yes. You won't believe it. She's had the place up for sale for several years now. When I talked to her, she took my first offer, no questions asked. You are now looking at the proud owner of 12 Main Street, the sight of Pride's very own soon-to-be bakery." She smiled and her whole face lit up. At that moment, he realized he'd do anything to see her smile like that again.

"Congratulations. It must be exciting to have the first step done. What is your next move?"

He leaned back and listened to her talking about equipment and building permits, hanging on every word she said. He'd never thought about what goes into starting your own business, but after listening to Sara talk, he now wondered how she'd find all the time to do everything she had planned.

"You're doing this all yourself?" He hadn't realized that

he'd moved closer to her until their knees touched and she stiffened.

"Yes, well." She looked around the crowded room, no doubt trying to find an escape. "I better go check on my sister." She started to get up, so he rose with her.

"I know a few people that could come in handy if you need help with some of the carpentry work." He smiled when she took a step back, so they weren't standing too close.

"Oh, that won't be necessary. I have connections in Pride, as well." She smiled and nodded towards a group of Allen's friends who were currently acting like fools over the new baby. Iian, Todd, Luke, and the proud papa, Aaron, were giggling as they hovered over George. They held up a small basketball outfit including the smallest basketball shoes he'd ever seen. Allen smiled.

Sara chuckled. "You'd think Lacey had given birth to a seven-foot boy with a basketball in his hands, ready to go."

He laughed. "Wait until they open my present. Aaron will get a kick out it."

She turned and crossed her arms over her chest. "What did you get him? Nothing as ridiculous as a basketball, I hope?"

His smile dropped. "Why? What's wrong with a basketball?"

"Well, nothing if you were giving it to a toddler, but a newborn?" She started laughing. "You gave George a basketball, didn't you?"

Now it was his turn to cross his arms over his chest. "Maybe."

"You haven't been around too many newborns, have you?"

He shook his head. "My sister has a few kids, but I wasn't around when they were little." He looked around as a loud roar came from the group of men, then Aaron yelled over to him.

"Allen, where on earth did you find the smallest basketball known to man?"

He shuffled his feet and smiled as his friends rushed upon him. He watched Sara relax and melt into the rush of his friends, looking very comfortable.

"Last week I made a trip into Portland to do some Christmas shopping and saw it in a toy store window."

Aaron patted him on the back as the group of men pulled him into an impromptu game of basketball right there in the living room. They had a few seconds of tossing the ball among the crowded room, all to cheers before they heard:

"You boys know better than to play ball in my house." Lacey was still sitting across the room, holding the very small and sleeping baby, George. Her voice didn't really need to carry across the room for the power and command to be heard. The group of grown men stopped tossing the ball immediately and hung their heads, even though their smiles were still in place.

Lacey looked beautiful sitting in a recliner in a pair of dark purple leggings and a large black sweater. Her short hair looked perfectly in place and her smile told everyone in the room she ruled the roost with love.

Aaron walked over and sat next to his wife and new son. Their three-year-old daughter, Lillian, crawled up into her father's lap, her curly dark hair bobbing up and down. They looked like a family taken right off the cover of a Hallmark card.

"They look happy," Sara said beside him. He'd forgotten she was still standing next to him; he'd been caught up in watching the family moment.

"Kinda makes you feel like you want to be a part of it all," he'd said and looked at her, focusing on her eyes. He watched them go wide and he could tell she was thinking about what he'd said, imagining them in place of Lacey and Aaron. The silence between them was almost deafening.

Just then Allison approached, carrying her and Iian's son, Conner. The boy was almost asleep in his mother's arms, his dark curly head resting on her shoulder.

"There you are." She sounded a little winded. "I have a few more details to discuss with you, if you have time." Allison looked between the pair of them, a slight smile on her lips.

Sara blinked a few times and focused on her friend. "Yes." She grabbed her friend's arm like it was a lifeline and made a quick excuse to Allen, then walked out of the room with Allison in tow.

He sighed and shook his head as Iian walked up laughing. "You did it now, Masters."

He narrowed his eyes and took the beer his friend offered him. "What?"

Iian clinked his beer against his. "Scared the girl away. But she's thinking about you now." Iian laughed. "Didn't know you had it in you."

"What?" Allen took a sip of the cool beer, beginning to feel a little frustrated.

"You know; I've known Sara all her life. I've never seen her look at someone the way she was looking at you just now." His friend chuckled.

Allen thought it was due to Iian being deaf, but the man had an uncanny knack of knowing what was going on with everyone all the time. Since he'd been in Pride, Allen had always used his friend's gift to his benefit. He'd always asked Iian to tell him what he thought of his new recruits if they had what it took to make it through the training. So far, the man had never been wrong.

"Yeah, well." Allen took another sip of his beer, then his friend patted him on the back.

"Good luck with that one," Iian said. "She can be a hellcat if you ever cross her." He shook his head. "Claws like a lioness." His friend was smiling.

A lioness? Funny, so far Allen had seen nothing in Sara that would make him describe her in that way. More like a scared kitten looking for a dark corner to hide in.

"John Timothy! Get off the ladder this instant!" Sara stood with her arms crossed. It was less than a week after Christmas and the third day since she'd taken possession of Allison's building on Main Street. No, she told herself, *her* new building. John Timothy, a local electrician she'd known since she was a child, stood on top of the ladder looking down at her. The man had retired less than a year ago after a major heart attack. His two sons were busy working in the back room.

"Now, Sara, I'm not quite through here."

"You are not supposed to be on that ladder and you know it. Don't make me call your wife down here." She watched him scurry down the ladder.

She sighed and dropped her arms. Her head was

hurting from all the banging the other men were doing in the back. The sawdust was causing her eyes to turn red and itch. "You need to go back over there and sit down. You said you were going to supervise and nothing more. Don't make me regret letting you through my doors." She was so focused on Mr. Timothy she almost didn't hear the chuckle behind her. Spinning around, she looked right into someone's chest. She knew exactly who it was and tried to not let out a sigh of frustration. She didn't need the distraction right now. Slowly moving her eyes up, she looked into Allen's eyes and saw he was laughing at her.

"I just stopped by to see if you needed any help. I didn't know you'd be scolding John here." He smiled and nodded towards Mr. Timothy. Allen looked good. How was it that a man could look so good in faded blue jeans and an oversized Coast Guard jacket?

"How's it going, Allen?" Mr. Timothy said as he climbed down the rest of the rungs on the ladder and walked over to shake Allen's hand.

"Can't complain. So, how's construction going?" Allen and Mr. Timothy walked further into the room, essentially ignoring her. They talked about the building and what they were doing to it to make it ready for her. She unfolded her arms and decided Allen would keep him entertained and off the ladder, so she could finish placing her orders. Walking back to the makeshift desk that held her laptop, she sat down, took another sip of her coffee, and got back to work.

There was still so much to do before opening day, which she projected would be the middle of January. The building had only needed some minor changes. Electric and gas needed to be updated in the back room for her ovens. A large island was being built in the middle of the room, so she had a large surface to work on. There was already a small office that she was just having them paint for her. It had a large window that overlooked the kitchen area. She would need a new desk and chair that would fit in the small area. In the front room, the main countertop had been cut in half so that the remaining space could house her large refrigerated display cases. Looking at her computer screen, she smiled at the four large cases she'd just ordered. Delivery was set for next Tuesday. She felt like dancing around to celebrate but knew there was still so much she had to do. Her mixers, ovens, and other utensils still needed to be purchased.

She'd hired a company in Portland to create her logo and the images she'd need for all her menus. She'd spent the last three days fine-tuning her menu items and had emailed them to the company. They'd promised a rough draft of her menus later that week. She'd opened accounts under her business name with all the distributors that she would need. It helped that she'd worked with each vendor before and knew where to go. Her first shipment of flour, butter, and eggs were going to be delivered later next week, which meant that the large refrigerators for the back room, which she'd purchased from a company in Portland, would have to be delivered at least a day earlier. Picking up her cell phone, she called to set up the delivery. Ten minutes later, her headache had tripled. It seemed that her order had been misplaced and they had no record of it. By the end of the call, she'd arranged for three oversized, professional-grade refrigerators to be on a truck just in time for her first delivery of food. Knowing it took a while for the units to get cold, she wondered if she should set her food order back a day.

Looking down at her schedule and the list of items she still had to accomplish, she decided she'd call tomorrow and set the delivery back. Right now, she had some more ordering to do. She had almost everything else she would need except the conventional ovens.

She'd worked with a couple of different brands in previous jobs as a baker, but her favorite by far was Vulcan. It hurt to spend the extra money, but she knew from experience that the ovens would pay for themselves in the low maintenance they would require over the next few years.

"Wow!" a voice said from behind her, causing her to almost jump out of her chair. Allen's hands came down on her shoulders as he mumbled, "Easy. Didn't mean to scare you." She heard him chuckle.

"You didn't," she lied. "I was just focused." She heard him chuckle again.

"Are you really going to pay that much for an oven?" He kept his hands on her shoulders, and she wished more than anything that he'd move them. She couldn't think when he was touching her.

"Yes, actually, I'll be getting two of them." She looked over her shoulder at him and tried to dislodge his hands. She only succeeded in making him move them a little so that now he was massaging her shoulders. She had to admit, it felt wonderful.

He whistled and shook his head. "What are those?" He moved his hand away from her shoulder long enough to point at her computer screen.

She turned back towards her screen as he continued to

massage her neck. Closing her eyes for just a second, she tried not to think of what his hands were doing to her system.

"Those are fryer baskets." She closed her eyes again and rolled her head forward.

"The kind you make French fries in?"

"Hmmm, yes."

"Why would you need fryer baskets?"

"Donuts."

He stopped rubbing her shoulders. "You're going to have donuts?" She sat up a little, straightening her back and looked at him.

"This is going to be a bakery." He was looking at the computer screen, then a huge smile crossed his face.

"What else are you going to have?" He pulled out a five-gallon bucket, flipped it, and sat on it next to her. The excitement was written all over his face, so much so that she couldn't help but smile at him.

"Well, if you want, I can show you my menu." She opened the file on her laptop and he leaned closer to her to get a better look.

When he was done reading over the simple menu, he turned to her and smiled. "You're going to have monkey bread! Sara, you are not only doing this town a great service, I think you've just stolen my heart." She knew he was joking, but it didn't stop her heart from skipping a beat.

CHAPTER 3

$\mathcal{I}$t felt like his lungs were on fire. Even when his body begged for air, he steadied his mind and continued to hold his breath for another fifteen seconds. When he finally came up for air, he noticed he'd been the last one to do so. It had always been that way. His new recruits were all treading water around him, some gasping for air, others easily swimming. He'd taken stock of who had come up first and the order that the other seven recruits had come up.

"Jones." He nodded towards the skinny kid. "Dry off, change, and be in my office in five. The rest of you, take ten laps and call it a day." He hated letting the kid go, but so far, his record wasn't impressive. You had to be made of stronger stuff and the hundred-and-thirty-pound twenty-two-year-old just didn't have what it took to be in the Coast Guard. Sure, he'd worked hard for the last three years, but that didn't mean he was tough enough to handle an open ocean rescue.

Allen dried off and watched his recruits swimming laps

in the Olympic-size swimming pool they used to train for water rescues. Finally, after a few minutes, he turned and walked towards his office. The kid was standing by his door looking like every other recruit had before he'd given them the news. The kid's shoulders sank, his head hung low, and he avoided eye contact with Allen.

He hated telling kids that their life's dreams were being squashed. Only once in the last several years had he been wrong about someone. Terry O'Brian had been much like the kid standing before him now when Allen had given him the news that he wasn't cut out for the job. Terry had taken it badly, but the next year had shown back up on Allen's doorstep, fifty pounds heavier with bulging muscles, and his head firmly on his shoulders. He'd passed the yearlong classes with flying colors and had gone on to take a position in Alaska, one of the roughest jobs along the coast. Allen smiled. Maybe this kid could bounce back like Terry had, he thought, shutting his door behind them.

When he got off work, he decided a meal at the Golden Oar was in order. Sitting in the familiar room with the sounds of a crowd and the smells of wonderful food always lifted his spirits. By halfway through his meal, he'd talked himself into believing that cutting the kid loose was for the best. If he looked at it from one angle, he could have just saved his life.

After he'd eaten, he sat there and chatted with Iian a little. When he left, the snow was coming down in thick clumps. Already his truck was starting to slide on the hill when he went up towards Main Street. When he saw the light on in the bakery and Sara's small car sitting outside, he pulled over and parked behind it. He'd hate to think that she'd have any more car problems on a night like this.

Sara stood back and watched as her new appliances were being hooked up. The vents and fans had been installed yesterday, and now the two ovens sat beautifully below them. The ovens, one a gas six-burner with two ovens below, the other a double-stacked, double-wide convection oven, looked perfect along the stainless-steel-plated walls. Her new register was sitting on the countertop, but she decided she could unpack it at the last moment. It was the same she'd used at her last job. The new coffee machine and espresso machines sat along the back counter, ready to use. She figured she'd try those out soon since she was dying for a caramel latte.

She still had so much to do in the front but decided to take a break and watch the process. Looking around the large back room of her bakery, she smiled. The light-yellow walls made the place look cheery. The shiny chrome worktables in the middle of the room gleamed in the daylight. She'd yet to unpack all her utensils; they sat in several boxes in the corner, out of the way. The huge mixer sat on the opposite wall. It was an older model that she'd found used online, but it looked and ran like new. The shelving that would hold her dry supplies still had to be put together. They sat in large boxes pushed up against the back wall. She planned on putting them together herself later that night.

Her sister stood beside her, looking bored. Becca had wanted to come down and help her today, but so far all she'd done was text her friends. It took the men less than half an hour to have everything set up. When she walked over and tested the units, they kicked on and she couldn't wait to bake something in them. She was still waiting for her refrigerators, which would line the wall to the left, but everything else had been delivered and setup. When the men left, she walked over and took one of the boxes from the corner and placed it on the worktable.

"Becca, you can help me out by unpacking my utensils. They hang on the hooks here." She showed her sister the hooks hanging above the workspace. "That box," she pointed to the other box along the wall, "is full of knives and they go on the magnets there." She pointed towards the long magnetic holders that hung above the cutting table. "Be careful, they are very sharp. I'm going to finish up front. If you have any questions, let me know."

She watched her sister set her phone down on the worktable and open the box. Becca still looked bored as she got to work, but she knew her sister would do her best to have everything in place.

When she walked back into the front room, she was greeted by the two-smiling face of Allison and Conner just outside the front door. She rushed to open it for her friend.

"Wow look at what you've done so far. The place looks wonderful!" Allison said as she wiped her snow-covered boots on the large mat that Sara had set out. It was just an overly large black work mat, but it kept the floors clean for now. She planned to buy a better-looking one for when she opened the doors.

"Thank you. Would you like a tour?" Sara reached over and grabbed Conner from Allison's arms. The little boy had his arms reached out for her and the second she held him, his chubby fingers reached up and intertwined with her dark curly hair.

"I'd love one." Allison hung her coat on the coat rack Sara had placed by the front door. She planned to replace it with hooks that would line the wall next to the door. For now, the coat rack and her small desk and folding chair were the only furniture in the large front room beside her display cases.

"Actually, maybe you can help me out." Sara turned to her friend.

"Sure, anything." Allison looked eager.

"I need some tables and chairs and possibly a couch for this room. I don't want anything new since I think most people in town appreciate a little history. I was planning on hitting the antique stores in Edgeview this weekend. If you have a free day, maybe you'd like to go with me, since it is what you did before you became a world-famous artist." Sara smiled at her friend.

Allison laughed. "World famous, huh? I'd love to go shopping with you. Let me text Iian and make sure he can schedule a day at home with our little joy here." Allison tickled her son's stomach and was rewarded with a fit of giggles. While Sara tried to hold the wiggly boy, Allison texts her husband and arranged it all.

"There, we're all set. Saturday, I'm all yours. I can't wait. I haven't been antiquing since...well, since I ran Adam's Antiques." Allison laughed.

"Do you miss it?" Sara set Conner down and watched him run circles around the room. Looking up at Allison, she saw a tear slip down her friend's face. "Oh, no. Don't do that." She rushed to her friend's side. "I didn't mean to make you sad."

"You didn't." Allison smiled. "Seeing this old place being fixed up, it does me good knowing that it will be used again. I have nothing but fond memories of this place. Of my parents and of Abby during happier days."

Allison's sister Abby had died; cancer had taken her quickly after they'd graduated high school. They'd lost their father a few years before, and Abby and Allison had pretty much taken over the family business. The antique store had shut down a few years back when Allison's art career had rocketed to huge proportions.

"I'm sorry." Sara knew what her friend had gone through back then.

Allison spun in a slow circle, much like her son was still doing. "It makes me happy knowing you're turning this place into something great again. It's sat empty for too long." She was smiling when she stopped. "I can't wait to see it all when it's finished."

Sara smiled. "Let me show you the kitchen. You'll get a kick out it. They just finished installing my stoves."

Allison picked up her son and they started walking to the back room. When she swung open her new doors, she was shocked to see her sister in a heated embrace. She recognized Nick Becker and coughed loudly, watching as the pair jumped apart. Hearing Allison giggle behind her, she straightened her shoulders and tried to stifle a smile. She needed to keep tighter reigns on her sister, as it was beginning to look more and more like her mother wouldn't do it.

"Becca, I'm sure Nick has other things he needs to be doing. I know you do." She turned to Allison, dismissing the couple as she started talking about everything that she'd done in the back room.

After Allison left, Becca made some excuse and said she was heading home, which left Sara alone in the store.

She didn't mind being alone. Actually, it was the first time she'd been left alone in the place since she'd taken possession.

She had a dozen or more emails she had to reply to. Her menus were completed, and she'd emailed the company with her approval and order. Her website was almost done, and she had emailed the designer a photo of herself. Now all she needed was pictures of some of her creations and an image of the building. She was waiting to take that picture until after her sign was delivered next week. Then there were the emails to her suppliers. By the time she was done, her head was a little dull and it was full dark outside the large front windows. She still had to put the shelves together in the kitchen and was excited to use the new tools she'd purchased just for this occasion.

She was about to shut her laptop down when she was notified of a new email. Opening it without a thought, she was shocked when an old image of herself crossed the screen. The picture had been taken almost five years ago, just after she'd moved away from Pride. Her hair was shorter then and she had an extra ten pounds on. But what shocked her and made her hands shake was that the image had been altered. Her head was pasted on someone else's body, a very naked body. Red splashes had crossed the woman's wrists and naked breasts. Her legs were at an odd angle, thanks to editing software. All in all, whoever had altered it had done a terrible job. But the meaning was clear. Sara's hands shook as she picked up her phone and punched the number she knew by heart.

"Detective Price."

"Hello, Detective. It's Sara. I just received another email."

"Sara? Are you okay?"

"Yes, I'm fine. There's just a picture this time."

"I'm sorry. Forward it to me if you would. Do you want me to send someone down there?"

"No. I'm fine. Besides, we already talked to Robert. He knows what's going on. I just thought I'd let you know before I sent this one to you."

"Thanks for calling. If you need anything, don't hesitate to let me know."

"I won't. Have a wonderful Christmas."

"You, too."

Sara hung up the phone and an image of Detective Price's face came to mind. The man was old enough to be her father. He had kind green eyes and more hair on his chin than on his head. But he'd been there for her the last three years as she'd dealt with the horrors of a madman.

Forwarding the image to his email, she looked at the image and frowned. She didn't remember having that picture taken of her. She didn't doubt it had been snapped at some party or even at her workplace. The more she looked at the image, the more frustrated she became. She'd hoped she had escaped all the madness by moving home again. But now, it looked like she was destined to be afraid for the rest of her life. Or until he finally made a move. Which according to everything the internet had to say about situations like this, they almost always did.

Just then there was a loud knock on the glass door, causing her to jump and scream.

"Sorry!" Allen said from the other side of the locked door. "I saw the light and thought I'd check on you."

She sat there, looking across the room at him until her heart settled back into her chest.

"Um," he looked at her and smiled. "Can you let me in? It's very cold out here."

She shook her head clear and rushed to open the door. "I'm sorry," she said as he stomped the snow off his boots. "You startled me."

He smiled. "It's okay. As I was saying, I saw the light and got worried. The snow's coming down pretty bad out there."

She turned and looked out the windows. She hadn't noticed that it had started snowing again. Since the sun had gone down, she'd tried to get as much work done as she could.

"Oh, it sure is. I only have a few more things to do, then I'll head home." She hoped he'd take the hint and leave. Instead, he took off his coat and hung it on the hook.

"Place sure looks different." He walked around.

"Yes, everything will be ready for opening day." She stood by the door, willing herself not to become too anxious. Then she spotted her laptop screen. It was still opened to the nasty picture. Walking over quickly, she slammed the screen shut.

He turned and looked at her, his eyebrows shot up in question.

"Is there anything I can help you finish tonight? I want to make sure your car starts this time."

"Oh, there's no need. Rusty put in a new battery and assured me everything else is fine."

"No trouble at all." He looked around. "What else do you need to finish tonight?"

She bit her bottom lip and thought of a million ways of getting him out of the building. But the thought of being alone in the building now caused a shiver to run down her spine. Images of past emails she'd gotten raced through her mind. Any company was better than going into the back room alone and trying to put shelves together all by herself.

"Well, I have these shelves that need to be put together."

"Shelves?" He smiled and clapped his hands together. "Sounds fun. Lead me to them. I'm an expert at putting shelves together."

An hour later, she stood over his bent head and laughed. He'd tried to cuss under his breath, but the fact that he'd been frustrated by simple metal shelving caused her to giggle.

"This should be simple." He tossed down the instructions. "It shows this bar"—he held up a small stainless-steel piece— "going into this slot." He pointed to the small hole.

Anyone could tell the two were not made for each other. The bar was twice the size of the hole.

"What are we doing wrong?" He looked up at her. The sleeves to his long shirt were pulled up, exposing muscular forearms dusted lightly with darker hair.

She shook her head. "It could be that the only instructions we have are in Spanish." She looked down at the pamphlet.

"Nope, I'm pretty good at Spanish. I think they sent us the wrong pieces. I mean, this doesn't even look like this." He pointed from the piece in his hand to the picture on the paper.

"Maybe we just need a break." She stood and stretched her arms above her head, working out any kinks in her shoulders and neck. Her legs were almost numb from sitting on the ground. They'd put the first two shelves together without incident, but the third shelf was different than the first two. This one would hold all her pans, so it was thicker and stronger than the first two that would just hold containers of dry goods. "What do you say to some coffee and a piece of pie?" She walked over to the small fridge that temporarily housed her food and looked at him, waiting for an answer.

"Sounds great." He looked back down at the instructions and frowned.

Smiling, she removed the pie plate and walked over to take down two small white plates. She'd been trying out new pie recipes at home during her spare time. Last night she'd made a Boston cream pie, but she'd yet to taste any of it. Grabbing two cups down, she walked over and poured coffee for both of them. Opening the drawer, she smiled when she noticed all the utensils were put away neatly. Just like her, Becca took great pride in doing a job well.

"Here." She handed him a plate and cup, then sat next to him again on the floor. "Maybe we are looking at it from the wrong angle." She tilted her head.

"What? Like upside down?" He scooped up a bite of pie and shoveled it into his mouth. She could tell he was about to say something but then stopped cold. His eyes shut, and he froze.

"What?" She waited for him to say something. Anything. Even after years and years of baking, she was always nervous when someone tried something she'd made.

When his eyes finally opened again, she could see the desire reflected there.

"Marry me," he groaned.

She laughed. "It's that good?"

"Better." He scooped up another bite and enjoyed it as well. She looked down at her piece and took a nibble. One of the hardest things about being a baker was keeping the weight off and critiquing your own work.

When the richness sunk onto her tongue, she tasted all the ingredients. Closing her eyes, she rolled her tongue around and enjoyed the burst of flavors. The richness of the chocolate, the sweet-tart of the cream. All in all, the pie was very good. Surely worthy of having on the menu.

Opening her eyes again, she was shocked to see Allen looking at her. His eyes were focused on her mouth. Thinking she'd left a dab of cream or chocolate on her lips, she quickly darted her tongue out to lick off any dribbles. When she did, she heard him groan. Then he set his plate down next to him and took hers. Without a word, he pulled her closer so that she was half on his lap.

"I tried to tell myself I didn't come here for this." He held his mouth an inch from hers. Her heart was beating so loud, she swore he would be able to hear it and feel it against his chest. The anticipation of the kiss was causing her to shake. Finally, he smiled a little and dipped his head towards hers. When their lips met, warmth spread throughout her entire body. She felt her toes curl in her shoes and wanted nothing more than to hold her body next to his for the rest of the night.

CHAPTER 4

She tasted like heaven and felt even better. Her breasts were pushed up against his chest and he could feel her breathing heavily. When she parted her lips, he dipped his tongue in for a taste and moaned at the richness there. Her hands went to his hair and held him close as his roamed over her hips, pulling her body next to his.

"You taste even better than the pie." He nibbled on her lips and let his mouth roam lower to her neck. When she leaned back, he took the opportunity to move even lower as she let out a low moan.

"I can't do this." She said lightly as she ran her hands over his shoulders. "I shouldn't be doing this."

He silenced her by taking her mouth again, causing them both to let out a low moan. Her hands traveled to his arms and she pulled back a little. "You make it so I can't think straight."

He smiled at her. "That's a good thing sometimes." He kissed her again quickly and watched her eyes close as she sighed.

"Sometimes." Then her eyes opened again, and he could see the fog lifting in them. "Right now, I have a full plate. I don't have time to stop and enjoy a relationship."

He sobered. "There's always time." She shook her head and pushed away from him, leaving his lap feeling cold and empty without her.

"I can't take the time. I can't take the chance right now. There's too much riding on what I'm trying to accomplish."

He thought about it and decided he might be rushing things a little too fast and nodded his head. "Fair enough. Are you going to the Jordan's Christmas party next week?" He held his breath.

She looked at him and tilted her head a little. "I was planning on it. Since I moved shortly before they started hosting them, I was looking forward to going."

She smiled a little and nodded in agreement. He felt like jumping up and down but nodded instead and picked up his coffee cup and took a sip. "You know, this doesn't mean I'm going to stop wanting to be with you, but the least I can do is help you finish getting your business together. And a good place to start would be getting this damned thing together." He smiled and watched her relax. "First things first. I'm going to sit here on the floor and finish the best piece of pie I've ever had." She laughed.

By the next afternoon the snow was melting so fast there was a rush of water flowing down Main Street. The town's streets had been built over a hundred years ago, so the drainage wasn't what it should be. Robert, the local sheriff, had the bad parts of the road blocked off, but the locals knew which other places to avoid.

Allen's team had gotten an early morning call about a fishing boat being hit by some rocks, but by the time they'd gotten there, the small vessel had righted itself and had waved them away. For the most part, locals knew that winter season was the worst, and most personal vessels were docked for the winter. It was the fishing and commercial vessels that Allen was mostly worried about for the next few months.

Storms could come up quickly. High winds and even the occasional huge wave could easily make the largest of boats look like a small toy. He'd seen it all since arriving in Pride. He'd been trained by the best and had trained some of the best himself. As a pilot, he usually waited for the storm out in the cockpit of his bird, but occasionally he'd get wet on a rescue. He liked the thrill of it, enjoyed knowing they'd saved lives. In the five years he'd been with the Coast Guard, he'd only lost three and they'd been long gone before he'd arrived on the scene.

When he'd driven through town early this morning, he'd seen the light on in the bakery. For the entire trip out to the training facility, his mind had been consumed by her. The feel of her, the taste of her caused his system to start working in overdrive. They'd finally gotten her shelf together around eleven last night and he'd followed her the few blocks back to her house. He'd desperately wanted to kiss her again but refrained from doing so. He knew she had a lot on her plate. Hell, he didn't know half of what it took to start your own business. He'd been here to oversee everything with the training facility, but there had been roughly a hundred contractors who were all getting orders from his commanding officers. All he'd had to do was babysit them and take over when the place was done. He was not only impressed by what she'd accomplished so far but the fact that she'd been doing it all herself made him realize that maybe she was made of stronger stuff than he'd first thought.

By the end of his shift, every muscle in his body ached. He was set to play another game of basketball the next day and knew he needed a break. Heading to the Boys and Girls Club, the only place in town that had a public hot tub, he checked in at the front desk and talked to Rickie, the teenage boy on duty for the evening. When he sank into the hot tub, his muscles started relaxing slowly. He could hear the rhythmic sounds of people swimming laps in the large pool beside the tub. Closing his eyes, he counted his heartbeats and waited for everything to slow down. He'd trained himself to control his breathing, control every inch of his body. It helped during those times when he was out on a save and most men would panic.

By the time he pulled himself out of the hot water half an hour later, his body was totally relaxed. Drying himself off, he almost passed right by her, but the dark streak under the water caused him to stop and watch. Her hair was tied back in a braid. Her long arms and legs carried her through the water quickly and gracefully in a practiced dance. He stood at the end of her lane and smiled when she stopped and looked up through dark blue goggles.

"Come here often?" He watched her pull the goggles off her eyes and saw surprise cross her face. She looked winded and her cheeks turned a nice shade of pink. He nodded towards the tub. "Just enjoying the heat a little. It helps with the day's bumps and bruises."

"Oh." She tried to smile. "I was just trying to wind down. Usually, a few laps help me clear my head."

He sat down on the edge of the diving board and rubbed the towel over his forehead. Water dripped from his hair, running down his chest, and he watched with pleasure as her eyes followed its motion like she was hypnotized by it.

"I was going to head someplace to eat after. Would you like to join me?" He held out a hand for her to take. She hesitated a moment then put her hand in his. When he pulled her out of the water, he smiled at the one-piece suit she was wearing. She wasn't built like a swimmer, more like a dancer. Her long legs and arms shined with the water glistening off them. Her hand remained in his for a moment, then she dropped her hand and walked over to retrieve her towel. He noticed she looked comfortable in her skin. She didn't try to cover her body and she walked with confidence. Shaking the water from her ears, she smiled at him.

"Actually, I put a pot roast on earlier. It should be ready right about now. What do you say to having a little home cooking? Of course," she chuckled, "you'll have to deal with my sister and mother."

He smiled. "I'd like to meet them. Sounds great. What do you say to meeting at your place in"—he looked down at his watch— "half an hour?"

She nodded. "If you can deal with my sister and mother, there might be another slice of something in it for you."

His eyebrows shot up. "Boston Cream?"

She shook her head. "Cheesecake."

He put his hands over his heart and closed his eyes.

"As I've said before, marry me." She laughed, and he knew at that moment he was a goner. Her hair was silky wet and falling in long curly wisps around her face. She didn't have an ounce of makeup on and he swore he'd never seen anything more beautiful than what he was looking at now.

Half an hour later, he approached her front door feeling like a teenager on his first date. His hands were sweaty, despite the frigid wind blowing off the coast. He didn't know what to expect from her sister or mother. He'd heard of them, but to be honest, he couldn't pick them out of a lineup, even though he'd probably passed by them a dozen times since arriving in Pride.

When the door flew open, he was greeted by a younger version of Sara. She was a lot taller and her hair was a few shades lighter. They had the same eyes and smile, but he could see something else in her eyes. He could tell that she usually got what she wanted. He remembered seeing her a few times on the beach during the summer with other kids from the school.

"Hi. Come on in. Sara's just putting the finishing touches on dinner." He noticed the house was spotless. Even though the furniture was older, it looked like it was in mint condition. The house smelled of cooking meat and potatoes, something he could appreciate. When he entered the small kitchen, he saw Sara rushing around preparing a salad. An older woman sat in a corner looking at a computer screen through glasses that sat at the end of her nose.

"Come on in." Sara turned and smiled at him. Her white apron looked clean and like it had just been pressed.

"Something smells wonderful." He smiled as he handed her a small bouquet of daisies.

"Oh, aren't these beautiful." She buried her face in the small bundle.

"They aren't much, just something I picked up at Patty's on the way up here."

"Come on and sit down. The food will be ready in a few minutes." She motioned to a chair at the table. He walked over and sat down. "Mom turn that thing off and meet our guest. Allen, this is my mother, Patricia." Sara introduced them once her mother walked over and took the seat next to him.

"Sara has told us so much about you. I can't thank you enough for helping her out with her car."

"It was no problem." He actually felt himself blush a little.

"I hear you're taking her to the Jordan's Christmas party, too," her sister piped in as she sat in the chair across from him. She folded her legs underneath her and leaned her elbows on the table and stared at him intensely. He nodded and tried to change the subject quickly as he adjusted in the hard chair.

Sara watched from the corner of her eye as her family tried to give Allen the second degree. Every chance Becca got, she would ask questions about his personal life. She doubted her sister cared that much about his personal life; more likely, she was just trying to get any scoop he might have. Finally, when Sara had set the salad on the table, she'd gotten bored and picked up her phone and had started texting someone.

"Do you need any help?" he asked, during a lull in the conversation.

"No, just finishing up the rolls. The pot roast pretty much cooks itself." She looked over her shoulder and smiled at him. He looked very uncomfortable at the small table with her mother and sister. Smiling, she turned back to the oven and pulled out the fresh rolls. She knew he was determined to keep trying with her. Well, if he was serious, he'd just have to make it past the crazy that was her family.

She'd never seen anyone eat as much as Allen could put away. The first bite he'd taken, he'd closed his eyes and moaned, much like he had with her pie the other night.

"I've never tasted anything better," he said as he helped clear the dishes. Her mother was back in her cubbyhole with the computer screen lighting up her face. She didn't exactly know what it was that her mother did on the computer all the time. She was a tax accountant, but Sara doubted she had that much work to keep her tied to the machine that long. Becca had disappeared to her room. The pair of them were pros at avoiding dishes.

When Allen started rolling up his sleeves, she jumped in. "You don't have to help. I'll take care of these later." She piled the plates on the countertop.

"Nonsense. It's the least I can do." He looked down at her doubting face. "Don't trust me with your good china?"

She smiled. "It's not that. You're a guest."

He shook his head. "My mother would have my hide if I didn't help out after having the best home cooked meal I've eaten since…" He tilted his head. "Well, I guess since I was back home." He smiled again and started filling up her sink with warm water and soap from the large container of yellow dish soap.

She watched for a minute as he started scrubbing the dishes then walked over and grabbed a towel. "Fine, but I'll dry and put them away."

They stood in the small space and worked quickly. It felt nice to have someone to help out. It didn't hurt that every time their arms would brush, or their hands would touch, she felt a burst of heat radiate through her. The spark would shoot up her arms and travel through her insides quickly. It was like touching a live wire, something she'd done once as a child. She'd been with Allison and two other girls. They'd decided to walk to the edge of town and see if they could sneak into an old barn they'd heard was haunted. None of them had known the fence surrounding the place was electric to keep the cows in the field. It had been just a quick painless jolt, like what she felt every time Allen touched her.

"Would you like a cup of coffee?" She dried her hands and dusted her slacks off.

"Sounds great. You mentioned cheesecake?" He walked over and sat at the table with a child's grin on his face.

"I suppose you'd like a large piece?" She pulled out the pan with her latest trial cake. It was an old recipe, but with a new twist. There was chocolate swirled around the top, and inside were two layers, one dark layer of mint chocolate and one of her normal cheesecake recipes. She set the plate down in front of him and nibbled on her lip and waited as he picked up his fork and carefully broke off a piece.

When he put the cake into his mouth, she watched his lips. A memory flashed behind her eyes of how those lips felt on her own. Trying not to close her eyes and moan, she moved her eyes back up to his and realized he was watching her with curiosity written all over his face.

"All I can say is that I've never had anything better. I want you to promise me that if you need a taste tester, you'll call me first." He scooped up another forkful.

"Really? It's good?" She waited. He looked up at her and set his fork down.

"Don't tell me you haven't tried this yet." When she shook her head, he scooped up another forkful and held it out to her.

"Trust me. I've eaten my fair share of cheesecake, being from a family that loves their desserts, but this is by far the best I've ever had."

She kept her eyes on him as she leaned down and took his fork into her mouth. When the richness hit her, it melted in her mouth and she smiled. Then she saw the heat in his eyes and noticed that he was watching her lips as she licked them for any crumbs. Time and space seemed to stop. Sounds came to a halt and even her heart seemed to take a break. How is it that he could do this to her with just one look?

Her mother's cough broke the spell. She'd forgotten she was sitting in the corner, witness to the event. When Sara looked over, her mother was still looking toward the computer screen. She blinked a few times to clear her mind of Allen and the images her mind had just conjured up.

"Mom, would you like a slice of this cheesecake?" Her mother turned to her and smiled.

"No, dear. I'll have some later. Thank you." She turned back to her computer.

Allen continued to enjoy his piece of cake. She was

surprised to see that it was almost gone. By the time she sat next to him with a small piece, his plate was clean and he leaned back in his chair and watched her nibble on her cake.

They talked about the bakery and Christmas. When he mentioned that he'd finished all his shopping and had sent all his gifts out already, she couldn't help being impressed. She'd only gotten her mother's gift so far. She still had a half dozen people to buy for.

"Do you have a large family?" She leaned back and took a sip of her coffee. It was lukewarm, but she didn't mind.

He shook his head. "Just my folks and my sister. My grandparents died when I was young. I have some cousins in Texas but have never really been close to them."

"Is your sister older or younger?" She realized she didn't know much about him.

"Younger by two years." He smiled. "Married her high school sweetheart. Jake went to the same boot camp as I did." She watched a frown cross his lips. "He was stationed just a few clicks from where I was in Iraq." He smiled. "They have a four-year-old and a two-year-old. Boys, both of them." He pulled out his phone. "She sent this last week."

When he was done flipping through his pictures, he turned his phone towards here. Two smiling faces looked back at her. They had on matching pajamas and were sitting in front of a large Christmas tree. They shared that smile with Allen, the eyes too. But instead of dark brown curly hair, they had bright white hair, bordering on translucent.

"They're beautiful." She smiled and handed him back his phone.

"Yeah. Dawn—that's my sister—spoils them rotten. So, do my folks. They all live back in Rockwood, my hometown in Maine."

"I've never been to Maine. I hear it's a lot like Oregon, but colder."

He smiled. "I'd choose Pride over Rockwood any day. Not that it was a bad place to grow up, it just wasn't as friendly as Pride is. I guess I've just grown used to being a part of something bigger than just me. Besides, I really enjoy my job."

She got up and took their plates to the sink. When she turned around, he was standing and putting on his coat.

"Well, I have an early morning, so I'd better get going. It was nice meeting you, Patricia."

Her mother turned and said her goodbyes. Sara followed him to the door, silently pleased that her sister was nowhere to be found.

"Thank you for the dinner and cheesecake." He stopped in front of her door, one hand on the handle. For a split second, she thought he was going to leave without kissing her. She'd thought of little else during the entire dinner. When he turned to go, she grabbed his arm.

"Allen?" He turned back towards her and she went up on her toes and placed a light kiss on his lips. "Thanks for putting up with my family." She started to pull away, but he took her shoulders and pulled her closer, claiming her mouth in a heated kiss that melted her. When he finally pulled back, she took in a gulp of air and realized her heart had kicked into overdrive.

He nodded and smiled, then turned and was gone

without a word. When the door closed, she heard a whistle behind her and spun to see her sister sitting at the top of the stairs, fanning her face with her hands.

"Wow, that was hot." She stood and came down the stairs.

Sara crossed her arms. "I guess it's only fair that you see me kiss since I've seen you suck face with little Nickie Becker."

"He is not all that little anymore." Her sister playfully shoved her.

"Yeah, I noticed." They giggled as they headed back into the kitchen.

CHAPTER 5

*S*ara felt like pulling out all her hair. Her new fridges were being delivered late, and her first shipment of food was sitting in the front units, which were not built to keep those items as cold as they needed to be. Now she was staring at a giant leak in the roof. The water dripped down on her clean worktable, causing a slight noise with each drop. The recent big snowfall they had gotten had all melted and the rain and sleet they had gotten last night had caused water to pool on the worktable and spill onto the floor. She'd pushed a bucket under the drip, and by the time Jack Timothy, John Timothy's oldest, had made it there, she'd had to empty the bucket three times. Jack had used a tall ladder to get up to the roof and look at what needed to be done. When he'd come back down an hour later, soaking wet, he'd informed her the entire roof would need to be fixed in the spring, but for now, he'd patched it up as best he could. Now she'd have to budget for a new roof. She hadn't been up there and wondered what it entailed. Was it flat or did it have a slope? She supposed she should have asked Jack, but right as he was leaving, the truck with her refrigerators pulled up in the back alley.

While the two men were unloading and setting up her units, she mopped up the water and cleaned her workbench. The men finished their task and left. She knew the units wouldn't be cold enough to put all the food into them yet, so she went into the front room and sat at her laptop. After she finalized the design for the sign that would hang on the front of the old brick building, she sent a few emails to her friends back in Seattle. She'd had a few close friends while working at some of the top bakeries in Seattle. Josie had been her closest friend for the last few years. The short Asian woman had more fire in her than Sara had known what to do with at first. Her friend's actual name was Jyotsna, but she preferred to go by Josie since she had moved to the United States when she was eight. They'd both worked for Seattle's West Bakery. At first, the two hadn't gotten along, but then after Stephan, the owner's husband, had hit on both of them, they'd banded together. After that, they'd gone everywhere together.

Sara looked at her email to her friend and smiled. She hoped that Josie would reply and prayed with all her heart that she'd say "yes."

Josie, I'm sorry I haven't emailed sooner. Bad Friend! I hope you had a great Thanksgiving, even though I know you don't really celebrate it. At least you had a day off. :) Anyway, I'm emailing to let you know I've finally done it! And no, I'm not talking about jumping out of an airplane. I'm opening my own bakery in Pride next month. Sara's Nook will be open for business around the middle of January. I'm dying for a few good employees, but will settle for you, if you're willing. LOL. There's a cute house for rent just down the street and I can't wait to get out of my mom's house. I think between the two of us, we could afford the rent. It's small, but in good shape. I'm sending you the address of the house and my shop so you can Google them. Please say yes, I'd die if I had to do this without you. Your wonderful tea cakes are what Sara's Nook needs! I can promise you at least what we made at SWB. I know it's a small cut from what you're making now, but everything is cheaper here in Pride. Call me. I know, I know. I should have called, but I'm too chicken. I'm afraid you'll say no and I think I can handle an email better than a call. But, if you're going to say yes, you can call me if you want. --Sara.

She read it over a few times and closed her eyes as she hit the send button. So far, she knew that Becca was going to be working part-time, but all her sister could do was stand behind the register and take orders. She needed at least two more bakers. She hated to seem desperate, but when the times called for it, she had no problem begging. Pride was a small town. For the most part, she knew everyone in it. She had a few possibilities for other workers but wanted to hold out and hear from Josie first.

She couldn't wait to see what the place looked like after she was done. She and Allison were set to go antiquing tomorrow. She was nervous about finding the right pieces. What if she didn't find anything? There were stores in Portland, but she hated to settle for something new.

She locked up for the evening and enjoyed the stroll back to her car. She'd taken to parking it across the street at Patty's. That way it left the parking spots empty just in front of the store. She was halfway across the street when she noticed her windshield. It had been perfect, with no cracks. Now, however, it looked like someone had thrown a brick through it. Rushing to her car, she stopped just in front. The glass was punched through completely in one section and a large gaping hole was letting all the water in as the light rain continued. She noticed something dark sitting on her front seat and rushed to unlock her door.

How could this have happened? The front windows overlooked the parking lot. When she finally had the door open, she looked down at a large chunk of stone. Turning, she looked at the side of Patty's building. Nothing looked like it had fallen off it. The tall stairs leading up to Amber's apartment looked sturdy. Sara locked her door again and walked to the front of the store.

Patty O'Neil was a larger woman in her late sixties. She wore bright colors and almost always had a smile on her face. Sara had always thought of her as Pride's very own welcome wagon. Patty was the person organizing all the get-togethers in town, although most people didn't know it. Sara had found out one day when she'd been coming out of the bathroom of the store. She'd overheard Patty on the phone with someone. She was busy telling the person who to call and what dishes they should bring.

When Sara walked into the store, Patty smiled and stopped her conversation with another woman. Ruth was as high society as Pride got. She was always meticulously dressed, and Sara had never seen a hair out of place on the older woman's head.

"Well, hello there, Sara. Ruth and I were just saying we can't wait til your bakery opens. Weren't we Ruth?" Patty looked to the other woman for confirmation.

"Yes, it's on everyone's minds what you'll be calling it." Ruth and Patty leaned forward a bit.

Sara smiled. "Sara's Nook."

"Oh, how wonderfully fitting." Both women smiled, and Ruth clapped her hands.

"Patty, I wanted to stop in and let you know, I think part of your building fell off and hit my car. I'm not a hundred percent sure, but it looks like part of the stone from the back wall."

"Oh, no! How dreadful. Are you alright?" The larger woman rushed over to where she was.

"I'm fine. It must have happened sometime during the day. I'm afraid it went right through my windshield, though."

"Oh goodness. Let's go take a look. Ruth, would you mind the store. Oh, and give Robert a call, would you. Just in case. He can take a look and make sure nothing else is loose."

Patty put on a large purple raincoat and grabbed a bright yellow umbrella.

As they stood in front of Sara's car, Patty shook her head and made a tsking noise. "It sure looks like that's what happened." Then she turned and looked at the side of the tall building. "How on earth do you suppose that happened? It doesn't look like anything is missing."

"That's what I thought. Wouldn't there be a hole somewhere?" They both stood there looking up into the rain at the side of the building. When a car pulled up they both greeted Robert, the local sheriff. Robert was almost ten years older than Sara, but they'd always gotten along well.

"Well," he looked at the old building and pointed his searchlight at the side of the wall. "I don't see anything out of place. But just in case, I'd hire an inspector to take a look first chance you have, Patty."

"Most definitely. Do you think the building is safe?"

"Yes, I see no reason to be concerned. It's just a small chunk." Robert pulled the piece out of Sara's front seat. "Do you have a garage to park this in tonight?"

Sara nodded her head. "I can have my mother park in the driveway."

"Well, my insurance will pay for the replacement. Just call Rusty and have him do it. Tell him to bill me and we'll take care of it all."

"I'd suggest telling everyone to park away from the building until you get it looked at."

"Of course. We're just lucky no one was hurt."

Robert turned to Sara with a smile. "Amelia and I can't wait until you open your doors. We've been dying for a good place to get a cup of Joe. Tell me you're going to have coffee." He gave her a pleading look.

"Several kinds." She smiled. "Free cup with a purchase of a piece of coffee cake for the first week."

He rolled his eyes and sighed. "Coffee cake!" He said it like a dying man. "It's been a long time since I've had coffee cake. We can't wait."

Just then, bright lights turned into the parking lot. Sara recognized Allen's truck and smiled.

"Well, if I'd known there was a party...What happened there?" He rushed from his truck and stopped by the side of her car.

"Well, either my car was hit by a meteor, or part of Patty's building fell off and hit it." She smiled. She watched Patty and Robert head into the store after they said their goodbyes.

He looked at her car and opened the door. Robert had set the large chunk next to the wall before he'd gone inside.

Now, she stood under her umbrella and watched Allen look up at the building with a frown. "Robert thinks it fell from the side?"

"Well, I don't know. But Patty's going to have the inspector out." She looked up at the side of the building for what seemed the hundredth time.

"Hmmm." He stood there looking up into the dark.

"You didn't have to stop. Robert cleared the glass from my seat. I'll be okay driving the short distance home."

"Huh?" He looked down at her, still a frown on his face. "Oh, no. I needed to buy some dog food." He turned back towards the building, this time searching the edge of the parking lot.

"Dog food?" She was shocked. She didn't know he had a dog. She supposed there was plenty about him that she didn't know.

"Yeah, Beast will need some. Probably a bed and toys as well." He continued to look along the wall.

"Beast?" She was getting confused. "I didn't know you had a dog."

"I don't." He smiled at her. "Well, you can't really call him a dog yet." He walked over to his truck. He'd left it running and the lights were still on. She could see in the brightness that the rain had stopped. When Allen stopped to open the door of his truck, she heard a high-pitched bark. Then he pulled away from the door carrying a small, dark ball of fur.

"Oh!" She rushed over to his side and they stood under the front awning of the store as the puppy, formally named Beast, licked her face and hands.

"He'll grow into his feet," Allen said smiling at her. She looked at the puppy's paws and saw what he meant. "Hence the name Beast. One of the guys I work with had a litter. He brought a few in today trying to get rid of them before Christmas."

She laughed. "What if he doesn't grow into them? You could end up with a petite dog." She laughed when the puppy tried to crawl into her coat. She unzipped it a little as he snuggled into her chest. "He's cold. I don't think Patty will let you take him inside. I can stand out here and keep him warm if you want to grab his supplies."

He smiled at her. "Are you sure?"

She nodded and watched him turn and go into the store. A minute later, Patty opened the door and smiled at her. "You can come in and at least stand by the doors. But no further." Sara stood just inside the doors with the puppy sleeping against her chest in her coat. Actually, Beast was keeping her quite warm.

Less than ten minutes later, Allen walked to the front with a cart full of items.

"Did you buy Patty out of all the dog toys?" She laughed at his full cart.

"No, actually it looks like someone beat me to it." He smiled. "She did have a full cat toy selection, though, and I thought Beast wouldn't mind." He frowned a little. "At least not this first time."

By the time Allen had checked out, Beast was fully awake again and trying to get down. "He probably has to go."

Allen clipped on the new collar and ripped open the leash. "Here, I'll just walk him in the grass." He set the puppy down in front of his truck and Beast decided to relieve himself right there in the parking lot. "Or," Allen said laughing, "right here is good." She laughed.

"I like that sound." He said, looking at her. She smiled back at him. "What do you say we follow you home? Make sure you get there okay."

She nodded and ruffled the puppy's ears when Allen picked him back up. The two of them looked good together. The shadows that crossed his face made him look a little dangerous, but the small puppy cradled in his arms made him look irresistible. They followed her home and she was glad they had. It was a little hard to see through the shattered glass. She was thankful for the assurance that he was there if she needed him.

When she pulled in, her mother's car was already in the drive and the garage door was open. Her mother and sister stood in the garage and watched her pull in. Allen honked his horn and waved as he drove by.

"Was that Allen Masters?"

"Yes, he made sure I made it home."

"Robert called ahead to make sure we knew everything was okay. Wow!" Her mother looked at the broken glass. "You're lucky you weren't in there when that happened. It would have landed in your lap."

Allen drove home thinking the same thing. He knew for a fact that the chunk of stone hadn't come off the building. He'd stubbed his toe on that same chunk last week when he'd parked at the edge of the lot. It had been sitting just on the edge of the parking lot in the snow. He'd been concerned that someone else would trip over it, so he'd un-earthed it and moved it further into the grass.

When he drove up his driveway, his neighbor, Robert, was parked next to his drive. Pulling in next to him, he rolled his window down.

"Hey," he nodded. They'd become friendly over the last few years since he'd purchased the place. Robert's house was about a quarter of a mile farther up the road. "Wanna come in for a beer?"

"Sure. Amelia's spending the night with her mother." Robert looked a little preoccupied.

"Anything wrong?" He stopped short of pulling the sleeping puppy from the car and looked at the local sheriff.

"Huh? Oh, nothing wrong between us, it's her mother's health. She's been in and out of the hospital lately. Amelia and the kids are staying with her tonight. Hey, is that a new dog?" Robert walked over to his truck door and looked in the window.

"Yeah, Marcus Engrim's dog had a litter. If you're looking for a new pet, he still has six of them to get rid of."

Robert whistled. "Six? The kids have been begging for a dog. I'll have to run it by Amelia first. Now that she's working full time at the vet, I don't know if she'd want to come home and deal with another animal." He smiled as the puppy half crawled and half jumped into his arms.

"Come on in. You get the dog; I'll get the food." Allen grabbed the large bag of puppy chow and tossed it over his shoulder.

Balancing the dog food, he opened the door and flipped on the lights in his mudroom. Setting the dog food down, he ripped it open and placed a small amount in the new dish he'd purchased. He filled another bowl with water and set it next to the food. Robert set the puppy down and Beast attacked the food, spilling more on the floor than he actually got in his mouth.

"Come on in. I'll grab that beer." They walked out of his mudroom. The house wasn't huge, but the large living room and the kitchen had sold him on the place immediately. The high ceilings and the wood pillars gleamed. The stone fireplace traveled up the full two stories, allowing the warmth to spread throughout the entire house. Above, two long balconies ran on either side of the living room. The master bedroom sat over the large kitchen with two smaller bedrooms and a bath on the opposite side.

Downstairs he had an office to the side of the living room and a smaller guest bedroom. All in all, the place suited him.

Handing Robert a beer, he leaned back on the marble counter and took a sip of his own. He thought he knew why Robert was here. He watched him and waited.

Robert took a sip and sighed, then looked out the window. "Rumor is it that you've been seeing Sara."

Allen chuckled. "Yeah, I thought it wouldn't take long to get around."

"Well," Robert turned back to him with a concerned look on his face. "Got any clue who'd like to throw a chunk of cement through her window?"

"I was wondering the same thing. That same chunk has been sitting in the parking lot ever since I arrived in Pride. I know Patty knows it's been there; I just can't figure out why she didn't want Sara to know it."

"Yeah, she knows it. The piece fell off the back of the building four years ago. Patty had the inspector out then. When we went inside, Patty told me she didn't want to worry Sara and that her insurance would pay for it, seeing as Sara is sinking everything she has into the bakery." Robert shook his head and took another sip of his beer. "Damned if that woman doesn't beat all." He smiled. "Something my grandpa used to say."

Allen laughed. "It could have been some kids."

Robert shook his head. "I've checked with the usual culprits. Joe and Dwayne were in Edgeview all day with their mother. Since you're seeing her, I thought maybe you'd heard more about the whole deal in Seattle. I've called the detective that's handling her case there, but just got his answering machine."

Allen stood up and set his beer down. "Her case in Seattle?"

Robert looked at him. "Oh, damn. I'm sorry. I thought for sure she would have told you." He shook his head and set his beer down. "Before you ask, it's not my place to tell you. I assumed you knew. I better get back to the house. Thanks for the beer." Robert started to walk toward the back door. "Oh, Allen, your new dog left you a little something back here. I guess you can call it a housewarming present." Robert chuckled as he walked out.

After cleaning up Beast's mess, Allen finished setting up the dog bed and toys he'd purchased in the mudroom. The puppy spent the next few hours sniffing around the house, trying to mark anything he could. Allen knew all too well how to train a dog and right before bedtime he placed Beast back in the laundry room and shut the door. Immediately the whining started, and half an hour later, he progressed to howling. By the time Allen was showered and sitting down to watch the evening news, the dog had fallen quiet. But when the TV turned on, the barking started again.

Allen walked over to the door and opened it. Beast sat on his bottom looking up at him with his tongue rolling out his mouth. There was a huge smile on the puppy's face if Allen had ever seen one.

"Fine, you can come out and watch the news with me. But no more messes on my floor. And you go right back in when I go upstairs to bed. Is that understood?" The puppy looked at him and then walked between his legs and into the living room.

An hour later, after cleaning up two more accidents, Allen headed upstairs and lay in bed listening to the puppy bark. He tossed and turned for the first half hour, then finally got up and brought Beast in bed with him. The small dog turned three circles then lay next to him on his giant bed and closed his eyes.

"Just this once, buddy. We are not going to make a habit out of this. I've got an early morning and you'll just have to get used to your new room." The dog looked up at him for a second, then went back to sleep.

Allen tried to roll over, but the eight-pound puppy was lying on his legs and felt like a ton of bricks. How is it he had the largest bed known to man, yet one small dog could take up so much room?

CHAPTER 6

"What about this one?" Allison stood next to a small desk in one of the largest antique stores in Edgeview. Sara walked over to it and looked down. The desk looked solid, but there were a few scratches on the top. Nothing that couldn't be sanded out. She didn't like the light stain either but supposed once she sanded it she could always stain it a darker color. The size was right and she liked the design. Taking out her measuring tape from her purse, she checked that it would fit in her small office.

"Yes, it's perfect." She smiled at her friend. "Now all I need is a chair." She looked around the room. "Maybe we can find something over there." Sara marked the desk with a yellow tag to show that the item was taken then followed Allison into a smaller room that had over a hundred old chairs.

It was just after lunch and so far, that morning they had already found four small, round maple tables for the front eating area, and two high-top tables that matched. Then she'd stumbled upon the perfect mission-slat-backed chairs. There had even been some higher ones for the high-top tables. She'd purchased a few extra chairs and decided to make a mock waiting area for custom orders.

Now all they needed was an office chair for her and a small table for just inside the door where customers could place their dirty dishes and silverware.

"Are you really going to make breakfast sandwiches?" Allison asked as she turned a chair around to get a better look at it.

"That's the plan. I've got this recipe for these yummy honey bread buns that go great with eggs and ham. I'll also have bacon and turkey sausage, but I like them with ham the best." Sara sat in a chair, trying it out, but when she leaned back, the entire chair almost fell over. Shaking her head, she got up and continued looking.

"What about custom cakes? Like wedding cakes? Have you done a wedding cake yet?" Allison looked eager.

"You're already married, silly." She smiled at her friend.

"Not for me." Allison rolled her eyes. "I spent weeks drawing my own wedding cake, but I found I just didn't have the talent for it." Her friend smiled and pointed to a dark cherry chair, the same color she'd been thinking she would stain the desk.

"Oh, it's perfect." They walked toward it, "Let's just hope it's as comfortable as it is beautiful."

When she sat down in it, she closed her eyes and sighed. This was what she'd been thinking of. Dreaming of. This was a chair she could sit and relax in for a few minutes and do some paperwork in. She held her breath as she leaned back a little, testing the chair out. When it leaned back smoothly and stopped short of tipping her out backward, she tried the swivel and was rewarded with a smooth ride.

"Perfection." She smiled at her friend.

"Good, now we can get all this delivered and go have a cup of coffee."

An hour later, they sat in Starbucks on the busy side of Edgeview. It was right by the hospital and the large windows overlooked the emergency room doors.

"I didn't know they'd opened this up here." Sara frowned a little. "Didn't this used to be a gas station?"

Allison laughed. "Yes, but shortly before Conner was born, they opened this up. It's in a perfect location, I think." Her friend looked out towards the hospital. "I was just here the other day." Allison chewed her bottom lip.

"Oh? Is everything okay? Nothing wrong with Conner is there?"

"No," Her friend shook her head and smiled. "We were getting an ultrasound."

"Ultrasound? You mean...you're pregnant?" When Allison nodded her head, Sara jumped up and hugged her.

"Oh, congratulations. How far? What sex? I'm asking too many questions." She laughed.

"I'm fifteen weeks. According to the ultrasound and the nurse on duty, we're having a girl. But Iian keeps saying it's a boy." She laughed as she pulled out her cell phone. "Maybe you can tell? I can never make heads or tails out of these pictures. Even the artist in me can't see anything but a blob."

Sara looked at the screen and could see clearly that Iian was right. "It looks like a blob to me. A wonderful, beautiful blob. I'm so happy for you two. Does everyone know?"

She shook her head. "Just the family. We figured we'd tell a few people and let it get out. So feel free to spread the word."

"If you wanted the word spread in Pride, all you'd have to do is mention it while shopping at Patty's." They both laughed.

"How do you think we told everyone we were pregnant the first time? Megan and I talked about it while buying diapers for Sara." They laughed.

"Is it true that you and Allen are an item?" Allison leaned closer over the table.

Sara rolled her eyes. "I knew Patty would spread that one around. I don't know what we are, but I can tell you I've never been kissed like that before." Sara smiled, then gasped. "Oh, that reminds me. He's taking me to the Christmas party this week. I haven't even gotten a dress yet."

Allison clapped her hands. "Goodie, dress shopping. I had a dress picked out, but I think I'm already too big for it." She held her hands over her stomach and Sara could see the small bump now.

"What do you say we stop by Jasmine's boutique? I bet they'll have the perfect dresses for us."

"Sounds great. I bought my prom dress there."

"So did I." Sara laughed.

By the time Allison dropped her off at home, she was exhausted. Her car had been picked up by Rusty first thing that morning with a promise he'd have it back to her by the next morning. She was dying to go into the shop but decided to try a new cupcake recipe she'd been tossing around. Her menu was pretty much set already, but she wanted to do weekly specials. She carried her new black dress and heels up to her room then got to work in the kitchen. Her mother was sitting in her usual spot, eyes glued to the computer screen.

"Mom, what do you do all day on that thing?" she asked as she pulled out the pans.

"Internet porn." Her mother chuckled when Sara gasped. "No, I'm just gambling your inheritance away, dear."

Sara stopped and put her hands on her hips and glared at the back of her mother's head.

Her mother turned around and smiled at her. "If you must know...As you know, I've been running my own accounting firm for the past few years. Well, I've gotten a couple of high-paying clients and at this point, I've been contacted by a company in San Antonio. They'd like to buy me out and I'm giving it some serious thought. I'm tired of sitting in this corner, working ten hours a day." Her mother leaned back and closed her eyes. "I want to be on a beach somewhere, with young studs handing me fruity drinks." Sara smiled and could just picture her mother harassing the staff.

"You should do it." She pulled out the butter and eggs from the refrigerator.

"Not yet. At least not until after Becca is taken care of." Her mother's smile dropped a little and she turned back around and started clicking on her keyboard.

Sara had never really thought about the responsibilities her mother must have faced alone. She'd always thought of her mother as a flake. Never really cooking a good, healthy dinner for her or Becca. She'd never thought that the reason was she'd been too busy working to take the time out. She'd never once asked her mother what she wanted.

"I'm sorry, Mom." Sara set everything down and walked over to kiss her mother's cheek. "We appreciate all that you've done for us."

Her mother reached up and patted Sara's hand, which rested on her shoulder. "I love you girls. I'm so proud of you for starting this bakery. Just don't let it get in the way of life. You're still young. You should have some fun while you can." Her mother's smile widened. "That Allen Masters looks like he could show you a good time."

"Mother!" Sara pulled her hand away and turned her back on her mother. She didn't want her to see her flaming cheeks.

"What? Just because I'm old doesn't mean I didn't see the sparks flying from his eyes when he looked at you."

"Really, you make him sound like some sort of demon." Sara laughed at the cartoon image of her and Allen, sparks and fire flying from his eye sockets when he looked at her.

Her mother sighed and turned back to her computer. "All I'm saying is take some time to stop and smell the roses. You'll regret not doing so when you're my age."

Her mother's statement played over and over in her mind a few days later as she balanced the large container of cupcakes, her laptop, her purse, and a steaming cup of coffee as she walked from her newly wind shielded car to the front door of the bakery. Juggling everything, she unlocked the front door and knew immediately something was wrong.

The sound of water running caused her to set every-thing down and rush to the back room. Her mind raced to images of the roof leaking again. What she saw when she got there shocked her to her core: The room was destroyed, and the back door was kicked in where someone had broken in.

Allen rubbed his eyes and took another sip of the terrible coffee. Three hours of sleep did not sit well with him. He was giving some serious thought to why he'd decided to have a dog in the first place. The drive into town was relaxing, but when he hit the outskirts of town, he noticed the police car and truck outside Sara's shop. Hitting the breaks, he pulled behind Robert's car and rushed into the building, leaving his truck running.

"Sara!" he called out at the door, running to where he heard voices coming from the back room. Stopping just inside the back door, he gaped at the mess.

There was an inch of water on the floor, most likely due to someone plugging the sink with paper towels and leaving it running. The faucet was turned off now, but the sink was still spilling over the sides. All the pans that had hung over the center workspace were tossed about; some were even dented. Her utensils were the same, some so badly, they no longer resembled what they had been. The shelves they had worked so hard putting together were tipped over and all the bins that held her flour and sugars were dumped out and causing a sticky mess in huge piles on the floor. The back door was shattered. The old wood had cracked under the weight of someone's foot.

Robert looked up and held his hand up to him. "Better not step in. It's a mess in here." He pointed to the wading boots he wore. "They clogged the drain in the floor with cardboard, so it would flood. Sara, go on out front. I'll finish up here and come out in a few minutes."

He stood back as Sara walked towards to him. She held herself rigid, her shoulders square, her arms crossed in front of her. Her tennis shoes were soaked as were the bottom few inches of her jeans.

"Are you okay?" He pulled her into the front room then engulfed her in a hug. Her face was blank, but when he held her, her shoulders slumped, and he heard her sniffle. "Let it go. I'm here," he murmured into her hair as she began to cry into his jacket.

He held her as she cried and when Robert walked out, Allen shook his head. He held back until Sara pulled away and wiped the remaining tears away.

"I think Robert wants to talk to you."

"Why don't you have a seat." He motioned towards her small makeshift desk and chair. She walked over and sat down, looking at her hands. Allen could tell she was embarrassed about crying in front of him and Robert, but she straightened her shoulders and took a deep breath.

"When was the last time you were here?" Robert pulled out his paper and pencil.

"Yesterday morning. I met Allison here. She drove us to Edgeview where we went shopping all day. I thought about stopping by last night, but Rusty didn't have my car back until this morning."

"The back door was kicked in and the lock was still engaged, so short of having an alarm system, you couldn't have done much. Does it look like anything is missing?"

Sara shook her head. "There was nothing of value taken. The most expensive items are my stoves and refrig-

erators. I didn't even have my register out of the box yet."
She pointed to the box sitting on the countertop. "They just
wanted to destroy everything."

Allen walked over and stood behind her and placed his
hands lightly on her shoulders. "Could this have anything
to do with what happened in Seattle?" He felt her stiffen as
she spun and glared at Robert.

"What?" He shrugged his shoulders when she just
continued to glare at him. "Alright. I mentioned it the other
night. I thought for sure you would have told him, after all,
you two are—" Robert cut his statement off when Allen
glared at him.

"No, this has nothing to do with what happened in
Seattle." She stood and crossed her arms over her chest.
"Now, if you're done in there, I have a lot of cleaning up
to do."

Robert nodded but put his hand out as she started to
walk by him. "I'm sorry, Sara. I shouldn't have said
anything."

She relaxed a little. "It's okay. Oh, have a cupcake on
your way out. They're right there in that box on the end of
the countertop. Take one for Larry down at the station and
everyone else." She walked into the next room. When the
door shut, Robert looked at him.

"She's pretty shaken up. I'm sure she'll come around
after she settles down."

He nodded and watched his friend open the box of
cupcakes. His eyes opened wide when he saw how beautiful they were.

Robert shook his head. "How am I supposed to eat a
piece of art like this?" He carefully pulled out a yellow
frosted one. The frosting was piled high and Allen realized

77

it wasn't just yellow frosting, but a yellow daisy, complete with a white face and bright yellow petals. He watched Robert pull back the paper and bite into it.

"A taste of springtime in the dead of winter." Robert shook his head. "I'm going to be fat three months after she opens up. Mark my words." He shook his head and walked out the door eating the rest of the cupcake.

Allen stood there for a minute looking at the door that led to the kitchen, then pulled out his cell phone and made a quick call. By the time he walked into the back room wearing his rain boots, Sara had her sleeves and her pants rolled up and was using a push broom to sweep all the water into the now unplugged drain in the middle of the floor.

"Go away. I don't want to talk right now." She continued to sweep, and he could see she was working the anger out.

"Too bad. It'll go faster with the two of us." He walked over and picked up a trash can and the dustpan. Doing the best he could, he scooped up the soggy flour and sugar and took them out back to the dumpster in the alley. When he walked back in, he bent to scoop up the next load.

"Iian and Todd are on their way here. They're going to stop by the hardware store and get a new door and alarm system." Sara stopped sweeping and gaped at him. "I know you don't want any help, but did you really think you were in this alone?"

After a minute, she shook her head. He watched a tear slide down her cheek. He wanted to go gather her up but knew she wouldn't want him to. Instead, he went back to his task of cleaning up.

Two hours later, he finished helping Todd install her

alarm system as Iian and Luke finished installing her new steel back door. Over three dozen people had stopped by offering their help. A large group of older women took charge of the rest of the cleaning, so Sara could focus on weeding through her utensils, deciding which could be salvaged and which were beyond help. Three of her large pans had dents in them, but for the most part, she'd been lucky. Her knives had been thrown at the wall, leaving large holes that the Timothy crew had patched, promising they'd be back in the morning to paint over the newly fixed spots.

"There." Todd dusted off his hands. "Let me show you how this works." He walked over to the panel and Sara followed him. "It's the same system we have at the restaurant. You put in your code like this." Todd punched in the code and there were three sharp beeps. "Now the system is armed. If anyone opens the front door or back door..." He walked over and opened the back door. Loud screeching noises came from the speakers they'd installed. Todd shut the door and hit the buttons to disarm the system. "It also calls the local PD." He smiled. "So, as long as you don't forget your code, you're set."

Sara smiled. "I can't thank you enough. Everyone. For all your help."

"These cupcakes are all the thanks I need," Todd said as he took another one from the box.

CHAPTER 7

*a*fter everyone left, Sara stood in her kitchen and looked around. Insurance was going to replace all the pans and utensils, but her heart hurt a little knowing someone had come in and purposely destroyed what she'd made. She knew who it was, well not his name or what he looked like, but she knew who had done this. The question was how had he found her? She'd thought that if she picked up and moved back home that the threats would stop, but it only seemed to speed them up.

"What are you thinking?" She almost jumped at the sound of Allen's voice behind her. She should have known he wouldn't have left with the others. Turning, she looked at him. He still wore his work uniform and large green rain boots. The sleeves on his shirt were pushed up and there was a drop of icing from her cupcakes on his shirt.

Shaking her head, she looked back into the kitchen. "I'm trying to not think of it as spoiled. Last time,"—she took a breath and decided to open up to him— "when he did this to my apartment in Seattle, he went through and touched my things. He didn't destroy them, just touched them, moved them around. I donated everything to Goodwill and bought all new clothes." She crossed her arms over her chest and remembered the feeling of being violated for months after the intrusion.

He walked up behind her and gently turned her around. "I'm sorry. I'd like to know more, but I can see you're tired."

She shook her head. "Weary, but not tired. I've gone so long without telling someone. If you want, maybe we can grab some dinner and I'll tell you about it."

"That sounds great. I'll drive." He smiled and pulled her into a light hug.

Sara locked up and walked out the front door, knowing her alarm was armed by the flashing green light. "Thank you." She turned to Allen as they stood outside the storefront.

"For what?" He pulled her close as they started walking towards his truck.

"For calling in the troops. I would have done it sooner or later after I'd worked off some of the steam. Thank you for taking the day off to help me clean up the mess, for being there and being a friend."

He stopped in the middle of the street, just in view of Patty's large windows and kissed her. When he finally pulled back, after hearing a honk and laughter, he smiled down at her and pulled her the rest of the way out of the road. "You're welcome."

Sitting in his truck with the heater on full blast, she relaxed into the warmth and watched the lights go by the window. She didn't know where he was taking her, but at this point, her head was too dull to care.

Feeling the truck stop, she opened her eyes and realized they had stopped in front of a house. "Is this yours?" She sat up and looked out the front window. His headlights only hit halfway up the garage. It was too dark to see anything else.

"Mine and Beast's." He smiled then got out and walked around just in time to help her out of the truck. "I thought you might like someone else to cook for you tonight."

"You can cook?" She stopped and looked up at him. His smile spread, and she felt her heart skip.

"I guess you'll find out." Instead of walking to the front door, he walked around the side and opened the door. A black spot rushed out between his legs. "Beast doesn't like his room." He shook his head and flipped on the outside porch light. They both turned and watched the small dog do his business in the grass. Then he plodded back towards them and started jumping at her feet. She bent and picked him up and was rewarded with kisses all over her face. She followed Allen into a good-sized laundry room. She saw the dog bed, food, and water were set up. There were toys scattered all over the floor.

"Sorry, I should have taken you through the front." He shut the door behind her, then walked over to scoop up a small pile of puppy poo.

"Did you poo in the house?" She giggled and snuggled with the dog.

"I'm glad you find it all so funny," he said when he came back from cleaning up.

"He'll get potty trained soon enough."

"I'm working on the rest of the house first. This is kinda his room. Tile is a lot easier to clean than carpet."

"I bet." She smiled and set the dog down and followed Allen into the living room. She liked the space and the colors he'd used. Light and clean. The fireplace was impressive, as was the sheer size of the rooms. He walked into the kitchen and rolled up his sleeves again.

"This will be a while. If you want, I have some old sweats you can change into. Your feet must be freezing."

She looked down at her wet shoes. The numbness had been there so long; she'd almost forgotten the discomfort. The thought of peeling off her wet jeans and shoes sounded like heaven.

"Sounds great. Actually, if it's not too much to ask, can I use your shower?" She rubbed her hands up and down her arms.

"Sure." He walked over to her. "I should have thought. You probably wanted to go home and—" She stopped him by putting her finger over his mouth.

"If I wanted to go home, I would be home." Smiling, she reached up on her toes and placed a soft kiss on his mouth. "Now, point me in the direction of hot water and those sweats."

What was he doing? He looked down at the pasta he was cooking and closed his eyes for a second. Sara was up in his shower, right now, naked and wet. And as far as he could tell, she had no plans of leaving for the night. Thank God!

"Okay, focus Allen." He told himself. "Or you'll burn the spaghetti. If you can't make the easiest dish in the world, she may change her mind about you and ask to be taken home." He shook his head clear of images of her in his shower, the bubbles from his shampoo running down her. Shaking his head again, he stirred the sauce.

Fifteen minutes later she walked down his stairs wearing an old pair of sweats from his SEAL days. They hung low on her hips and she'd rolled them several times to allow her feet to poke out from the bottom. The large t-shirt she wore matched the pants and hung halfway down to her knees.

She'd tied her hair up in a loose ponytail. Her face was clean, and she had never looked better.

"Mmm, something smells wonderful. Spaghetti is my favorite dinner." She leaned against the counter and watched him.

He felt nervous all of a sudden. So much so, he almost burned the rolls he'd heated up.

"Can I help?"

"No, just sit there and look gorgeous." He waved towards the table, which he'd already set with his good china that consisted of two plates that matched and two non-plastic glasses. The salad he'd tossed from a pre-made bag sat in the biggest bowl he had.

He watched her hips sway as she walked over to the table and sat down, crossing her legs underneath her. She looked over at him and smiled, and he realized she knew he'd watched her.

Two could play at this game. While she'd been upstairs, he'd quickly gone into the mudroom and pulled on a clean shirt and pants. Walking over, he bent slowly and pulled the bread from the oven. When he looked again, he smiled, knowing her eyes had gone a little cloudy as she'd watched him move.

By the time he sat at the table, the food laid out in front of them, he was so worked up, he doubted he could take a bite. And if he was a good judge of her, he knew she felt the same way.

"Allen?" She sat there looking down at her food, not touching it.

"Sara?" His throat had gone dry. Then she was in his lap, her body next to his, her mouth on his. His hands gripped her hips as her fingers dug into his hair, pulling him closer. He shoved up from the table, knocking over the chair as he turned and pushed her against the wall, holding her still as his hands snaked under the shirt to touch her soft skin.

She moaned when his fingers brushed over her, causing her nipples to pucker. Her head fell back, exposing her neck as he slid his hands down and started to undo the string of the sweatpants.

"Are you sure?" he tried to say, but it ended up more as a moan.

She nodded her head over and over, then yanked his shirt over his head. She moaned when her eyes fell on his chest, then she pulled him closer and kissed him again. His fingers went under the wide waist of the sweats and he found her wet and ready for him. He almost stopped breathing as she started making little noises as he rubbed her. Then she was trying to yank his jeans off his hips.

"Hang on, just hang on. Let me think." He tried to pull back.

She shook her head quickly. "No, now. No thinking." She licked her lips and watched him from underneath her eyelashes. He would have done anything she'd asked at that moment. Pulling out the condom he'd shoved in his back pocket, he yanked down his jeans. He came back to her, holding her against the wall, his palms flat on either side of her head as he hovered over her lips. He ran his fingers down the side of her neck.

"It appears you have entirely too many clothes on." He smiled and watched her eyes close.

He slowly pulled her shirt up, exposing her navel, then pulled it up even more as he exposed the soft skin over her ribs. Finally, when he'd pulled the shirt over her head, he leaned back and took in her beauty.

"Beautiful." He ran a fingertip over her soft skin. "I've never seen anything so beautiful."

"Allen, I'm burning up." Her hands were beside her hips, flexing on his wall.

"Let me take care of you." He leaned over and placed his mouth on her delicate skin. Her fingers gripped his hair as he tortured her with his mouth.

"Please," she begged over and over.

He'd worked himself up so that when he opened his eyes, there was a haze over everything. She still wore his sweats and in one quick move, he had them pooled at her feet on the floor. He sheathed himself quickly and pushed inside hers. Twin moans sounded as he flexed his hips against hers.

"Sara," he groaned as he held still.

"Please." She gripped his hips and dug her nails into his back. "Please, Allen."

He flexed and held his breath as they rushed to the finish together.

Sara listened to Allen's heart beating against her head and sighed. She was propped up against the wall of Allen's dining room, with a naked man holding her up. There had never been a more perfect moment in her life.

"Food's getting cold," he mumbled against her hair and she couldn't help herself, she laughed.

"With all this heat in the room, it's a wonder everything isn't burnt." He chuckled, then leaned back and placed a kiss on her nose.

"If you want to clean up…" He motioned towards the bathroom. She quickly pulled up the sweats and looked around for her shirt. She wasn't embarrassed of her body, but after cooling down, she'd realized the large windows in his living room were uncovered. She didn't know how close his nearest neighbor was.

He saw her looks and laughed. "Robert and Amelia's house is a quarter of a mile that way," he pointed towards the fireplace, "through very thick woods."

She smiled and found her shirt. "I'll be just a minute." She rushed off towards the bathroom.

After dinner, she stood by the back sliding door as he tossed the ball to Beast in the backyard. The little dog didn't really get the whole bring it back thing yet, but Allen enjoyed chasing him in the light from his deck.

He started a fire in the fireplace and they made love again on the soft carpet. She fell asleep in his arms, wrapped in his warmth.

When she woke, the small dog licked her face and barked.

"No, Beast," Allen said and snuggled his face deeper into her hair.

"I think he needs to go out." She giggled as the dog licked her face again.

"Yeah, probably." He groaned as he got up off the floor. "Remind me why we slept on the floor when there's a perfectly good king-size bed upstairs?"

She laughed. "Because it was so very romantic." She pulled the small blanket he'd grabbed over her and rolled over to look out the windows. "Oh look." She sat up. "It's snowing." She stood up and wrapped the blanket around her as he walked to the back door and opened it for the dog to rush out. Beast stopped dead when a snowflake landed on his nose. The tiny dog spun in circles and chased a few flakes before finally relieving himself, then he continued running around, chasing fat snowflakes.

After dressing, Sara convinced Allen to let her cook breakfast. When he came down, freshly showered, the cinnamon French toast was done. He swore it was the best he'd ever eaten. She was beginning to think he was biased. She quickly dressed in her clothes from yesterday, which Allen had thrown in the washer and dryer last night after dinner, then they headed into town. She had a mighty urge to bake.

When they got to the shop, everything looked better than it had last night. The building sat gleaming in the sunlight. Gone were the images of destruction from yesterday, replaced by the warmth of knowing the whole town was behind her.

"Are you sure you don't want to head home first?" Allen said when they stopped in front of the store.

Shaking her head, she smiled. "No, I've got an early morning delivery." She looked at her watch and figured she had just enough time to open up before the truck would be there. "Besides, I have a few recipes I need to fine tune."

"Anything involving chocolate?" Allen's eyebrows rose, and he had a hopeful look on his face. She laughed.

"Stop by around noon. There should be something for you to try out." She leaned over and kissed him quickly, but his arms came up and snaked around her, holding her tight and deepening the kiss until she was breathless. When she finally pulled back, she could see the heat in his eyes. She didn't know what she was going to do; she was quickly becoming addicted to him.

"I'll try to make it today. If not, we're still on for the Christmas party, right?"

"Of course. I even bought a new dress yesterday." She smiled. Thinking about the event caused her to get excited. A real fancy party. Here in Pride. She couldn't wait to see what the Jordan clan had done with the restaurant. She'd heard that Amber, their new manager, had made some major changes. He nodded and smiled as she jumped out of the truck, past the water flowing in the gutter. Turning around on the sidewalk, she waved as he honked and drove off.

When Sara walked into the building, she closed the door behind her, making sure to disarm her new alarm, and took a deep breath. She felt like dancing but settled for a quick twirl. When she entered the kitchen, she looked around. Yes, now the place gleamed and shined again. It felt like hers again. Flipping on the lights, she walked around pulling out everything she'd need for the day. Halfway through preparation, the back doorbell rang. Looking through her new peephole, she saw Zach, one of her deliverymen. She had heard somewhere that he lived in

Edgeview and had all the local routes. It was always a good idea to treat the deliverymen with kid gloves. If they liked you, you had an in to some of the freshest products. Opening the door wide, she smiled.

"Good morning, Zach. Beautiful day isn't it?" His smile wavered as he balanced the handcart with her boxes of supplies.

"I heard about the break-in yesterday. Is everything alright?" He looked around, a frown on his face when he stepped inside.

"Oh, everything is fine now. We cleaned it all up. They did some damage, but it's all fixed." She motioned to the patched wall.

"Yeah, I guess." He set the handcart down. "Had to replace a lot of your stock, though?"

"It's just food." She signed the paper when he handed her the clipboard. "My next delivery will be on schedule. I appreciate you fitting me in today."

He shrugged his shoulders. "No problem. I'm stopping by the Golden Oar to make a large delivery this morning. I guess they're having a big party there in two days."

"Yes, I can't wait to go. This will be my first year attending their Christmas party."

"That's cool." He looked around, avoiding her eyes. "I suppose you already have a date?"

Her smile almost faltered. She'd never really thought of him in that way. He was probably five years younger than her, but in her eyes, the age wasn't a problem. He was skinny, tall and looked like he hadn't grown into his body yet.

"Yes," she tried to think of something, anything else to say.

"That's cool. I guess I'll see you around." He started wheeling the handcart out.

"Zach?" She waited until he turned. "If you're done with your deliveries around noon, stop by. I'll have a batch of cupcakes ready. You can take a box if you want." She watched his face light up.

"What kind?"

"Well, I'll be baking Red Velvet, Strawberry Cream, and…" she paused for a moment trying to decide, "… Death by Chocolate." She smiled.

"Sounds good. I'll stop by on my way out of town." He turned and left, whistling on his way out.

Rolling up her sleeves, she started unpacking the boxes of supplies, then took her time filling her canisters with fresh flour, sugar, and cocoa. Dusting her hands, she pulled on her large apron and looked around. Everything was back in its place.

"Now, time to get to work." She started making the batter for the Red Velvet cupcakes first. It was an older recipe she'd discovered years ago. It was one of her favorites and would be used for cakes, tea cakes, and cupcakes. She had several batters that transcended like this one. Today, however, she was only making a small amount of the batter. Mixing the ingredients in a small mixing bowl, she smiled when she turned on the mixer for the first time and watched the ingredients swirl and combine. She flipped on her ovens, letting them warm as she prepared the other two batters. The containers she used to hold the batter were almost full two hours later. She looked at the clock on the wall and realized she still had time to make something more. Deciding on cookies, she started a batch of chocolate chip and peanut butter.

She had just finished with that batter when the back door-bell rang. Wiping her hands, she let Jack Timothy in, so he could finish patching the spots on the wall that he'd repaired yesterday.

By noon, when Allen showed up, she had two batches of each cupcake ready, and three batches of cookies, hot from the oven.

He walked in with three other men and a young woman. "It sure smells good in here. I hope you don't mind, I bought a few recruits along. We were heading back from beach training and thought we'd stop by."

She smiled. "No, not at all. The more taste testers, the better." She motioned to the display cases, where she'd put the cupcakes. "Choose your poison." It was wonderful having a dry run of serving customers. The espresso machine hummed as she made their orders.

She handed out freshly printed menus to everyone as they all sat on the folding chairs she'd placed around the room.

"The tables and chairs are being delivered tomorrow." She smiled, apologizing for the lack of space. A few people walked by the window and poked their heads in, asking for a sample. She handed out her last cupcake right as Zach walked in the door.

"Oh, looks like I was too late." He frowned.

She smiled. "Not at all." She rushed to the back and took the box from the countertop. Coming back into the front room, she set it down. "I put these aside for you." She opened the box and showed him the mixture of cupcakes she'd saved for him.

"Wow, thanks." He smiled at her. She felt eyes burning into her side and looked over to see Allen frowning at the kid. She felt like laughing but decided she'd explain every-thing once they were alone.

Finally, when the room was empty except for Allen and his recruits, he pulled her into the back room and kissed her, pushing her up against the wall behind the door. When he pulled back, he looked down into her face.

"What was that all about?"

"Hmm? What?" She tried to pull him down for another kiss, but he pulled back a little.

"Paying off your delivery man?" He smiled.

"More like bribing." She smiled back at him. "A girl does what she must for fresh eggs and blueberries." He chuckled.

"If I didn't know any better, I'd say the kid was hot on you." He pulled her closer.

"Yeah, he tried to ask me to the Christmas party." She bit her lower lip.

"He'll get over it." But there was still a frown on his face.

"What?" She put her arms around his neck and looked at him. "What has you frowning?"

"Nothing." He tried to wipe the frown from his face. "Just something Robert said, that's all. Well, Sara's Nook looks like it will be a successful opening week." He changed the subject quickly.

"Hmm, yes. I can't wait. Now all I need is furniture and employees. Not to mention the signs." She started thinking of her list and knew there was still so much that needed to be done.

"Don't worry. You'll have plenty of time to get the rest done." He kissed her again quickly. "I've got to get back. My schedule is pretty packed for the next two days. If I don't see you in between, I'll pick you up at your place at seven for the party."

She nodded and reached up to kiss him again. When everyone left, the place felt empty. She pulled out her laptop and started doing some ordering she'd been putting off. Her phone rang and when she looked at the number, her heart skipped a beat.

"Hi, Josie." She was greeted with a high-pitched screech.

"Oh my God, Sara. I'm so excited! I can't believe you're doing it. Yes. Yes. Yes. Count me in. I'm sorry it took so long to get back to you. I lost my cell phone and I dropped my Mac. I've been unwired for two whole weeks until I finally got my replacement phone." Josie wasn't usually this unconnected. Sara had taken her friend's silence as an answer of no.

"Really?" She took a large gulp of air and felt her head spin. "You'll really pick up and move to Pride?"

"Yes!" Josie screamed in the phone. "I'm packing as we speak." She heard her friend laugh. "I've waited for the right moment to tell Stephan and Bethany off. Things have gotten a lot worse since you left. I'll tell you all about it when I get there. It shouldn't take me more than two weeks to have everything tied up here."

"I can't wait. I'll look into renting the house today. I'm so happy you're going to be here." Sara closed her eyes on a wave of happy tears. Everything was falling into place. An image of Allen's face popped into her mind.

CHAPTER 8

The day was hell on him, and it had nothing to do with the three calls he'd gone out on and the long hours of training he'd put his new recruits through. Being apart from Sara had left his house feeling empty and his body craving hers.

He was sore in places he hadn't used in years. Even though he was used to the hard work and the long hours, he was looking forward to the next few days off. Morale around the facility was high. Everyone was looking forward to having some time off. The morning of the party came, and his phone went off just as he was getting out of the shower. Tripping over Beast, who was lying on the shower mat, he barely answered the phone in time.

"Hello?"

"Allen, it's Richard. We have a call for help in international waters. Sounds like a boat of immigrants ran into some bad weather."

"I'll be there in ten. Have them prep the chopper, and call the on-duty team?" Allen shoved out of the bathroom, racing towards his gear. Less than five minutes later, he had Beast locked up and was heading down his drive. Punching Sara's cell number, he waited as it rang.

"Morning." She sounded so cheery he almost forgot what he was racing towards.

"Hey, sorry to spring this on you, but I've got an international distress. I may be a little late tonight. What do you say we meet there?"

"Oh, I hope everything is alright." He heard the concern in her voice. "Sure, I understand. I'll see you there."

"Thanks." He drove by her shop and saw the lights on. "Don't tell me you're baking at this hour."

He could tell she was moving around, "Of course. Baker hours start early. Lacey contacted me earlier this week and ordered a few things for the party. Cakes, cupcakes, some fudge." He heard her sober up. "Be careful out there."

"Will do. Bye." He hung up and made it to the parking lot just as Marcus and two other men on his team drove up. They may goof off during off hours, but today they were all business.

Less than ten minutes later, they were flying over the water at top speeds. Dispatch squawked in his ear, giving him the latitude and longitude of the vessel's last-known location. His team was strapped in behind him, each doing their jobs, preparing for rescue. Each time they went out, they geared for the worse, not knowing what to expect.

It took them a little under an hour to reach the last known location. The weather out here was worse than on shore. Here the waves kicked up ten to twenty feet. The rain was coming in sideways and he could see lightning off to the north. Larry and Marcus scanned the horizon, looking for any sign of a vessel.

"There, two o'clock." Allen glanced and saw the smoke of a flare and the flash of its fire. He pointed the bird in that direction.

When they got there, he assessed the situation. Roughly three dozen people were crammed onto the smallest sailboat he'd ever seen. No one had life vests or heavy jackets for the cold rain that was pelting them. When the waves hit the small boat, he held his breath, hoping that it wouldn't capsize.

"Call it in," he told his copilot. "Have them get as many boats out here as possible. We're going to need them."

With the Coast Guard boats on their way, Allen and his team just had to continue to assess the situation and wait for backup. They wouldn't swing into action unless an immediate rescue was needed. Looking out his window, Allen saw everyone on the small boat start pointing off to the left. "Man overboard," he called into his radio. "Damn it. Find him." He glanced around, swinging the helicopter to the left quickly. Every team member searched the choppy waves for any sign of life.

It took them two minutes to find the mother and daughter bobbing in the cold waves, their dark heads barely hovering over each wave.

"You're on the rope, Marcus," Allen called to the back, signaling who would take the lead. Larry was the newest member of his team and had yet to make a water rescue. He couldn't afford to lose the precious cargo because of a rookie mistake.

Allen carefully positioned the helicopter with the

instructions his crew gave him as Marcus started moving down the wire with the basket. They were geared for the water in thermal wetsuits. Larry talked calmly into the radio, telling Allen when to move when to hold still.

"We've got them. Bringing the basket up now." Larry sounded happy. They were halfway up when a gust of wind caused the chopper to dip dangerously. He held the stick with both hands and for a second, his mind flashed back to five years ago.

"Man down. Man down," Larry screamed into his ear.

Sara looked at her reflection in the mirror and smiled. "Wow, you look good, sis," Becca said from behind her. Her sister was dressed in green leggings and a large Oregon Duck's sweatshirt.

"Thanks." She turned and gathered her long coat. "Don't wait up." She smiled as she walked out.

Running through the snow, she entered the Golden Oar and shook off her umbrella. Her heels were just a little wet as she walked through the doors. She was greeted by Iian and Allison. They both looked so wonderful, Allison in her new dress, Iian in a tux.

Soft Christmas lights hung from the ceiling, making everything glow and look magical. There was a huge pile of presents underneath a large Christmas tree which sat by the fireplace near the back wall. She handed her gifts over to an employee who took them and set them amongst the others.

Looking around, she noticed a huge fish tank where there used to be open space. The tank, complete with blue lights and exotic fish, looked great as it separated the bar area from the main dining room.

Employees were handing out drinks to guests and she grabbed a flute of champagne.

"Where's Allen?" Allison walked up behind her, wrapping her arms around her.

"Oh." She turned and hugged her friend. "There was a call. He should be here shortly." She nibbled on her bottom lip, hoping.

"Well, come on in and see what they've done to the rest of the place." She smiled and motioned her into the back ballroom.

A large Christmas tree stood in the center under a disco ball. There was a band playing on the stage, and people were slowly dancing around the tree to Christmas music.

Luke and Amber were already there and just seeing how they looked at each other made her heart skip.

"They look good together," Allison said beside her.

"Yes," she sighed and looked towards the front door. Iian walked over and, smiling, pulled his wife onto the dance floor. They look good together, too, she thought. Now she was left standing in the doorway, watching the couples spin in circles around the floor.

She was just turning around to walk back to the bar area when the music stopped short. Turning back into the room, she watched Luke get down on his knee.

"Will you do me the honor of moving in with me?" he asked a very embarrassed Amber. He opened a box and presented it to her.

"Yes! Yes, I'll move in with you." She laughed as he stood up and they hugged.

They spun around to the cheers of the crowd. But then

Amber pulled away. "Actually, now that I think about it. No."

The whole room went quiet. Every eye was on the couple. "No, I won't move in with you. Not until you say that you'll marry me."

Several people laughed. "She beat him to it," Aaron said to Lacey a few feet away from Sara.

Luke smiled, then got down on his knee again, holding up another box to her. "I was hoping to ask that question next." He opened the lid and smiled up at her. "It was my grandmother's." He pulled the ring out of the box and slid it smoothly onto her finger. "Amber Kennedy, will you move in with me? Be my family? The mother to Jackie? And to some human babies maybe a few years down the road? Will you marry me?"

Amber smiled and nodded, then the couple was kissing, and everyone cheered. Sara smiled as she watched the newly engaged couple turning around the dance floor. They looked happy. Marriage. It was a huge commitment; one she wasn't ready for anytime soon. But an image of Allen popped into her mind. Stepping back, she turned and walked towards the bar area and took another flute of champagne. She'd set hers down somewhere and had lost track of it.

"Here alone?" She spun to see Zach leaning against the bar.

"No, I'm waiting for my date to arrive. For the moment. I thought..." She broke off, embarrassed.

"What?" He stood up and walked towards her, caging her between the fish tank wall and him. She hadn't realized that he was almost a foot taller than she was. Even though she thought of him as skinny, he still was bigger than her.

"You thought that since you turned me down, I wouldn't show?" He leaned his hand on the wall behind her, caging her in even more.

She shook her head and looked around. At this point of the party, everyone was still in the back room congratulating Luke and Amber and few people had trickled out yet. "No, I thought you'd find someone else to bring along." She tried to move around him, but he grabbed her. Since her dress was strapless, his cold hands curved around her shoulder, causing her to shiver.

"No, there's no one else." He leaned closer and she could smell the alcohol on his breath.

"Zach, I really think you should..." She moved his arm away then stepped aside.

"There you are." Allen walked into the bar area, causing Zach to jump back a full two feet. She let a sigh escape her and quickly walked over to him, not looking back at Zach.

"Are you okay?" He took her arm and steered her towards the main dining room. Looking behind him at Zach.

"Yes, just a misunderstanding." She felt warmer, close to him. His arms moved around her, and he smiled down at her.

"You look beautiful." He stopped and leaned down to kiss her.

"Thank you. You look very dashing." He did, he looked like a young Clark Gable, stepping into his next movie set or a high-roller Hollywood party. "How did the rescue go?"

His smile fell away. "Marcus fell from the bucket. He's

got a broken collarbone, but other than that...Thirty-five Mexican immigrants are alive."

"Oh, no. Is Marcus the one that had the puppies?"

He chuckled a little. "Well, his dog Sadie did most of the work, but yes. His wife and kids are at the Edgeview hospital with him now. He'll be fine." She could see something in his eyes.

"It wasn't your fault." She took his hands and held them in hers.

"For a minute there I was back in Afghanistan." He shook his head, then looked down at her and smiled. "None of that talk tonight. Tonight, it's all about dancing, good food, champagne, and presents." He pulled a box out of his jacket pocket. The long black box had a bright red bow on it.

"Merry Christmas." He smiled as she took it from him.

"Oh, wait here." She handed the box back to him and walked over to the tree, looking quickly for his present Finding it, she rushed back over to him.

"Here, Merry Christmas. Let's open them together."

"Okay, come over here." He steered her towards the fireplace and they sat on the stone seat in front of the heat.

They opened the gifts together.

She opened the lid to a dainty bracelet full of silver spoons, pans, cupcake pans, a small mixer, a rolling pan and even a whisk. She laughed. It was perfect.

"I saw it and thought of you." He smiled at her. "There's even a measuring cup." He set his box down and helped her put it around her wrist. The silver of the bracelet shone in the lights, sending sparkles around her wrist.

"It's perfect." She smiled at him. "Now, open yours."

He picked up the box again, this time ripping the paper off quickly. "I always love the sound of that."

He opened the tissue paper and stared down at her gift. The knife set was one of the finest, made for the highest quality restaurant. "I noticed you didn't have a good set the other day. These are the best." She smiled.

"You bought me knives?" He smiled at her and shook his head. "Leave it to a baker to buy a guy something he'd been thinking of getting for the last few months." He chuckled. "Do you know how hard it is to cook a steak without a good knife?" He pulled the box open and started looking at the knives one at a time.

She laughed. "Now you won't have to. I hope you like them."

He set the knife he was currently examining down and pulled her closer. "They're perfect." He kissed her and the heat from the fireplace wasn't the only heat in the room.

"Tell me you can stay with me tonight?" he whispered into her hair.

She nodded. "I packed an overnight bag." She pulled back and smiled at him.

"Good. Now,"—he looked around— "you mentioned something about bringing some fudge?" She laughed.

CHAPTER 9

*H*e'd never had a better weekend in his thirty-two years. They'd spent most of the time inside getting to know one another but had also taken a long walk in the woods behind his house, walking the dog and playing in the snow. He spent an hour on the phone with his family, enjoying the fact that they'd gotten his presents on time.

Sara ended up spending two nights. She'd convinced him to drop by the bakery the first day, just for a few hours. She had to make some calls and promised to bake him a large chocolate cheesecake. He couldn't resist.

Her tables and chairs had been delivered and were heaped up along the south wall. He helped her unstack them and they spent an hour moving everything around until she was happy with the placements.

"I've got some white tablecloths that will go over them. That small table,"—she pointed to a rectangle table—"goes to the right of the door. There will be a trash can to the left and people can clear their own tables." She crossed her arms over her chest and looked around the room, nodding her head. "Allison is going to hang some of her art along that wall." She pointed to the bare wall, across from the one full of refrigerators.

"What's going to go in those?" He pointed to the large display units.

"Cakes, pies, sandwiches." She tilted her head. "Party trays, salads. The cupcakes, cookies, and tea cakes will all go up here, along with some of the smaller specialty items."

He turned to her and took her shoulders. "Sara, just one question." Her face turned serious.

"Yes?"

"What exactly is a tea cake?" She laughed at him.

"It's a cookie made out of cake batter, covered with a thin layer of icing."

Looking around the place, he could just imagine it all finished.

"When are you opening?"

"I was shooting for the fifteenth. My best friend, Josie, is moving down from Seattle to work for me. I still need to find two more employees. One part-time, who will work when Becca is in school, and one full-time baker." She chewed her bottom lip and he knew she was already thinking about other things she had to accomplish.

"So much goes into running a business." He shook his head. "I would have never thought."

She smiled at him and walked across the room to wrap her arms around his neck. Her lips were an inch from his when Becca walked in the front door.

"Oh, hey." Her sister didn't even look embarrassed about catching them in an embrace. "Did you hear that

Amber and Luke are having an engagement New Year's party?" Becca texted as she said this.

"No." Sara pulled away and looked down at her phone as a message came in. She smiled. "We're invited. It's an 80s theme." She laughed. "Luke says you should dress as Tom Selleck since you're his twin without the 'stache. Actually," she tilted her head and looked at him, "when I first saw you, I thought you looked a lot like him myself."

He chuckled. "I've heard that before." Becca looked at them.

"Who's Tom Selleck?" They both looked at each other and laughed.

After leaving the bakery, Allen stopped by Marcus's place to check up on him. The man's whole family was crowded into the small living room. Marcus was propped up on the couch, watching football. He stayed for an hour, then headed out. Knowing the man was going to be okay helped ease the guilt that he still felt. By the time he headed to the Boys and Girls club for a weekly game with the guys, he was pumped for the rematch with the teens who had almost whooped their butts a few weeks ago.

When he walked in, the guys were all standing around, no doubt waiting for him.

"Sorry, went to check up on Marcus. He's doing fine. He's back home and on the mend."

"That's good to hear. We heard it was a bad fall." Aaron shook his head. "I wasn't on duty at the hospital that night, since I'm still out on maternity leave." Aaron smiled quickly. "But I heard they were overrun with immigrants with hypothermia." He shook his head and frowned a little.

"Yeah, it was a long night for everyone." He turned to Luke. "So, getting hitched, huh?"

Luke's smile doubled. "You're coming to the party this Friday?"

"Yeah. I'm not sure about Tom Selleck, though." He frowned. He really just wanted to wear something normal.

"No," Iian shook his head and stared at him. "We all have to do what our wives tell us, and since I have to go dressed as Ace Frehley, according to Allison, then you have to go dressed up as well." He crossed his arms over his chest.

Allen shook his head. "One big difference...I'm still a bachelor."

Iian and Aaron shook their heads. "You're seeing Sara. You have no choice but to dress up."

"What does that mean?" He frowned a little.

Todd laughed. "Sara is the queen of costumes. You wouldn't think it to look at her, but the girl has more costumes than a costume shop. Every year for Halloween, costume balls, or even school plays, she always outdid everyone else."

"She actually walked around one year in a big plastic bubble when she was dressed as the good witch from the Wizard of Oz."

"Glenda," Aaron piped in. When everyone looked at him funny, he shrugged. "Lacey loves old movies. We watched it a few weeks ago."

"Well, whatever. She had a huge ball dress, white wig, and a wand, and she rolled around town in that thing. It was great." Todd smiled.

Before Allen could reply, a group of teens walked in and all through the game, as they were getting their butts handed to them by kids half their age, Allen wondered what else there was to discover about Sara and why he was looking forward to finding out.

Sara looked at the fake hair in her hands and smiled. It was going to be perfect. Her outfit was already in the shopping cart when she'd spotted the fake mustache from across the room. She hadn't planned on buying Allen's costume, but everything was there. The Hawaiian shirt, the big sunglasses and now the mustache. She stuck them all in her cart.

If he decided not to wear them, she told herself, she wouldn't mind. Dressing up was one of her guilty pleasures. Most women had wine or chocolate. She didn't like the taste of wine and since she was around chocolate all the time, it just wasn't that desirable to her.

By the time she made it back to Pride, full dark had settled in. The small town's lights welcomed her as she drove through the side streets. She'd met with the elderly woman who owned the house that she and Josie were going to rent. Since Josie was absent and couldn't sign the lease, Sara had put everything into her name and paid the deposit. She'd worked it out that Josie's deposit would come after she'd gotten her deposit back from her landlord in Seattle.

Now all Sara needed to do was move in some furniture and wait for Josie to arrive, which would be after the new year.

When she drove up to her house, she noticed a shadow cross the side of the house. Shutting off her car, she stepped out and yelled.

"Nick, you'd better run home before I tell your mother you were sneaking around here." When Nick's head popped out of the bushes, reminding Sara of a whack-em game, she almost laughed. "Why don't you just ring the bell next time." She grabbed her bags and started towards the house.

"Don't tell my mother." Nick rushed over to her, helping her with her bags. "She doesn't know I'm seeing Becca tonight. I'm…" He looked around. "I'm kinda grounded."

She laughed. "Well, since you're helping me in with these"—she held up her bags— "I suppose I can let it slip this once." Before they made it to the front door, Becca opened it and looked out wearing very short pink shorts and an almost see-through white tank top. Sara stepped in front of her. "No, you don't. Get back inside right now and put some clothes on. Nick can't stay, anyway." Sara turned towards Nick, whose eyes had almost popped out of his head. "Goodnight, Nick." Sara grabbed her bags and shut the door in his face, then turned on her sister. "Just what do you think you're doing?"

"What was Nick doing here?" She looked innocent, but Sara knew better.

"Listen, that probably works with Mom, but I've been in your position before. Having boys over here, dressed like that"—Sara waved her hands up and down her sister — "will only get you one thing. You don't want to go down that path at your age. Not yet." Sara picked up her bags and walked into the kitchen.

"Oh, hello, dear." Her mother turned and smiled at her. "How was your shopping trip?"

"Beneficial. Want to see what I bought?" Her mother

stood and walked over to the table. She had always loved her eccentric taste in costumes.

The next day, she gave Allen his costume when he stopped by for lunch. He'd actually laughed and looked pleased when she told him that he could wear comfortable jeans with the shirt.

"The mustache might get a little itchy, but after a while, I bet you forget it's there." She smiled up at him.

"If all I have to wear is a Hawaiian shirt, sunglasses, and a fake mustache, I guess I'll survive." He pulled her closer, "So, what are you going as?"

"Oh no," she shook her head. "You'll just have to wait and see." She went up on her toes and placed a kiss on his mouth. "But I can promise you, you are going to love it."

"Does it involve fishnet? I don't know why it ever went out of style." He shook his head and she laughed.

"I'll give you that much. It does involve some fishnet." When his eyebrows shot up and a large smile crossed his face, she laughed.

"Amber stopped by earlier and ordered almost everything on my menu." She laughed. "My second gig and I haven't even opened. I'll spend all day today and tomorrow baking." She smiled.

"Just wait until you open. Birthday parties, graduations, weddings...I'll bet you'll be very busy."

"Hmm, hence the need for more employees." She frowned.

"Well, I'll let you get back to work." He pulled her up for one more kiss that left her thinking of him while she finished her work. By the end of the day, she had two employee prospects. To be safe though, she posted a "help wanted" sign on the front door. By the next evening, she had three more names to add to her list.

Since she had to arrive at the party early to deliver all the goodies she'd baked, she'd told Allen she'd meet him there. Becca had agreed to help out and before leaving the bakery, they had taken their time changing into their outfits. Getting all the boxes into the back of her car was a pain and she gave serious thought to buying a small van for deliveries.

When they arrived at Luke's house, Nick was standing in the driveway and he helped them carry everything in, after which, he and Becca had quickly disappeared.

She set up everything with Amber's help and ran her car back home, just a few houses down. She walked back and was just sitting down to a drink when the first guests started arriving. She stood back and enjoyed seeing all her friends and the other townspeople dressed up, enjoying themselves.

Half an hour later when Allen walked in the door, she held her breath at the sight of him standing in the doorway. How had she ever gotten the attention of someone so kind, so generous, and so good looking? He was every bit the part that he looked tonight. Strong, handsome, the protector. What had she been thinking? How had she let things escalate this quickly? More importantly, what was she going to do now that she knew she had really fallen for him?

CHAPTER 10

*a*llen walked into the room to a bunch of cheers. People slapped him on his back, laughed, or just shook their heads at him. He didn't like all the attention but smiled and kept walking farther into Luke's house.

He'd looked around the crowded place for Sara, but so far he hadn't seen her. He saw all of his other friends and had even spotted Becca, but no Sara.

"Hi," someone said behind him. He turned thinking it was Sara but instead stood a woman dressed as Cyndi Lauper. If he hadn't known better, he would have sworn it was Cyndi Lauper standing there. Her half-yellow, half-red hair stood in spikes. Bright colored makeup covered one eye and half her cheek, and her lips were a dark shade of purple. Beads of every color hung around her neck and wrists. Her tank top was net and her skirt flared out. When he looked down at her legs and saw bright pink fishnets, his eyes flashed back to her face.

"Sara?" She smiled and he could see it was her. How could he have not known it was her with that smile?

"Wow." He smiled back at her and slowly started walking around her. His eyes traveled every inch of her outrageous outfit. "Best costume ever." He crossed his arms over his chest and smiled down at her. "You even look shorter."

She smiled. "I'm wearing flats. Usually, I wear something with a heel. I don't know. You're rocking the Tom Selleck look. If I didn't know better, I'd say you were his twin."

He grunted and took the beer someone offered him. "Yeah, well."

"Don't you like dressing up?"

"Love it." The sarcasm rolled off his smile. "I hear you're really into it, though."

She nodded and smiled again. "I guess I've always had a thing for dressing up. It started right after my father left. He took off with Mom's best friend a week before Halloween."

"Ouch." He shook his head. "I'm sorry."

"For?" Her eyebrows rose.

"The stupidity of some in my gender." He smiled and took a swig of his beer. He hadn't heard about her dad.

"Well, anyway, that Halloween, walking around in my strawberry shortcake costume, all my worries, all my sadness disappeared. I guess you can say every time I dress up; I get that feeling back."

"Well, then, let's not waste it." He set his beer down and took her hands. "I hear music in the next room. What do you say we go enjoy the night?"

She laughed as he pulled them into the next room. He'd only been to two other costume parties in his life, and neither of those could touch this one. By the time midnight rolled around, everyone was crowded into the two largest rooms in the house. Everyone cheered at the end of the countdown. He pulled Sara into his arms and welcomed the new year with one of the hottest kisses he could remember.

By the time he walked her to her house, just a block over, most of the other guests had already left. The streets were empty as a light snow fell, making the world seem cut off and silent.

"It's so beautiful here." Sara stepped back and wrapped her arms around her chest as flakes landed in her hair. She started turning slowly, enjoying the rush of air. "I'm so happy that I came home." When she stopped spinning, he gathered her into his arms and gently pulled the wig from her head. He wanted to see the snowfall on her dark hair, to feel it in his hands.

"I'm so happy you came home, too." He leaned down and kissed her lips. Her purple lipstick had worn off halfway through the night and he'd ripped the damn fake mustache off his lip after his first beer. Now, her lips tasted like heaven and felt like silk. His fingers moved into her soft hair. When she wrapped her arms tighter around him, she moaned, and he felt her shiver.

"You feel so good." She pulled back and smiled at him. "I don't know what I did to deserve you."

He pulled her close and started walking towards her house again. She was a little drunk, and he was sure it was close to freezing out. Her long, dark coat kept out a lot of the cold, but still, he didn't want her to catch a cold.

"Why Pride?" She stopped and looked at him.

"Pardon?"

"Why did you move to Pride? There are Coast Guard stations everywhere. What made you stop here?" She

117

looked up at him, her dark hair getting matted with the wetness of the snow.

"To be honest, I'm not really sure. When I was stationed in Afghanistan, and our chopper went down, I had a dream of a beach. The first time I stopped along the Oregon coast, I knew I wanted to stay." He smiled and put his hand in hers, gently getting her to walk again.

"It is beautiful. Have you been to Haystack beach?" She tugged on his arm.

"No. I've heard about it, but haven't made the trip yet."

"Oh, maybe we can go someday." She sighed and started swinging their arms as they walked. When they finally stopped in front of her front door, underneath the protection of the front porch, he pulled her into his arms again and this time enjoyed a slow kiss that he was sure had steam rolling off his skin.

He pulled back when he felt her shiver again and watched her disappear into her house. He walked back to his truck in the snow and finally cooled down by the time he drove up to his house. He parked and knew immediately that something was wrong. The mudroom door stood at an odd angle.

Jumping from the truck, he rushed into his house and was rewarded with a low growl from Beast.

"It's okay, buddy." He flipped on the light and saw the small dog cowardly shivering in the corner. Allen punched in Robert's number as he went around the house flipping on the lights. He could instantly tell the place was empty. When Robert showed up, he was standing by the back door, waiting.

"Nothing's missing," he said and opened the door further. "I think they busted in the back door and when

Beast greeted them with a growl, they must have taken off."

Robert filled out a report and walked through the house, just in case.

"Well, I'll help you fix the door. They busted the lock, but if you want, I have a spare one in my trunk. Always carry a new one just for cases like this."

"Thanks. I'll go grab my tools."

By the time he finally got to bed, there were fewer than three hours before he needed to get back up and head in for his morning shift. His mind refused to shut down. Images of Sara kept popping into his mind. Her taste was still on his lips. She had seeped into every pore and he had become addicted to her, and he didn't know what he was going to do now.

The day arrived when Josie was coming into town. Sara stood in the doorway of their new rental house and waited. Finally, Josie's car turned the corner, followed closely by a small moving van. When her Neon stopped, Josie jumped out and Sara rushed forward to hug her.

"I can't believe you're here." She jumped up and down. Josie followed her movement and said, "I can't believe I'm here." They both did circles, laughing.

It took the moving company less than an hour to have the truck emptied and, three hours after Josie had arrived in Pride, their house was complete.

"I don't have a lot of furniture yet, but I'm sure we can get things as we go." Sara stood back and looked at the small space. Josie had a couch and chair, and a small flat-screen TV that fit just right in the living room. They didn't have a kitchen table or chairs yet.

Sara had her bed from her mother's house and most of her bedroom set. Josie had a larger bed, so she took the main bedroom.

"Here." Josie handed her an envelope. "I got my deposit back. Rickie tried to argue with me about a stain on the carpet, but when I pointed out that in my lease it said they'd carpet clean after I moved out, he gave it all back to me." Sara smiled. Her friend was almost six inches shorter than she was and weighed probably half of what Sara did, but Sara knew better than to try and cross her.

"He had no chance going up against you, trying to rip you off. Silly mortal." She smiled when her friend struck her favorite Mortal Kombat character pose.

"Liu Kang fears no one." She bowed.

"Is Liu Kang hungry?"

"Starved." Josie smiled. "But first, I want to see your bakery. I'm dying here!"

"Okay, okay. First, Sara's Nook. Second, the Golden Oar."

Five minutes later, Sara unlocked the front door and punched in her alarm code.

"Wow." Josie stood in the doorway and gaped. "This is perfect." Her friend spun around, taking in the entire room. "Now, I must see the kitchen." She held her arms up, like someone who was sleepwalking and started walking towards the backroom.

Sara laughed and followed her.

"O-M-G!" Josie rushed around, looking at everything. "You got Vulcan's! Oh, look at this." Josie rushed to her refrigerators next. She spent the next five minutes opening every drawer, looking in every appliance. When her friend pulled out a spoon that was bent, Sara walked over and took it.

"Oh, sorry. I must have missed this one. I forgot to tell you about the break-in. Well, it wasn't really a break in, more like kids making a mess. At least I've come to think of them as kids."

"What happened?" Josie asked, just as Sara's stomach let out a loud growl.

"How about I tell you over lunch?"

When they walked into the Golden Oar, Josie sighed. "I'm going to love living here. You know," she said as they were seated in a table right off the water, "I've lived in the city most of my life and just last month, after I lost my cell phone, I realized it wasn't all that bad being cut off from the world. Those two weeks without my phone or computer were the most peaceful I've had in years." She looked down at her menu. "I'm thinking of getting rid of them permanently."

Sara laughed. "You could really live without playing Mortal Kombat every day?" Sara shook her head. "I don't think so. By the way, what did you do for those two weeks? And don't tell me you went without."

Josie looked down at her menu, avoiding eye contact.

"Josie?" Her friend looked up at her with a smile.

"Fine. I went to the library every night." Sara laughed.

Just when they were finishing up with their lunch, a familiar face showed up. She hadn't expected to see Allen walk in the door with a pretty blonde. Both of them had huge smiles pasted on their faces. The shock of seeing the couple must have shown on her face.

"What? What's wrong?" Josie looked over her shoulder and tried to find what was causing Sara pain.

"Nothing." Sara tried to make herself smaller so that he wouldn't notice her. How could she have been such a fool? There was no way a man like him would ever commit to someone like her. She was a child compared to him. He probably had a new woman every month. There were certainly enough in town to keep him busy. Her chest hurt a little and her eyes were beginning to water. "Let's just go." She watched out of the corner of her eye as the couple took a seat at the bar area. When they disappeared behind the fish tank, the very same one he'd kissed her against just over a week ago, she tossed money down on the table and quickly walked out the door.

She should have known. What was she thinking?

When they were finally in their own house again, Josie stopped her from going into her own room.

"Okay, are you going to tell me what that couple has to do with you looking like someone took a sword to your chest? Who was that?"

She sighed. "Fine." Knowing her friend wouldn't let it go any time soon, she sat down on the couch and folded her legs underneath her. Grabbing the throw pillow, she hugged it to her chest.

"I've been seeing him, Allen, for a few weeks. I thought it was exclusive. Apparently, I was wrong."

Josie sat down across from her. "That scum bucket!" She got back up. "I'm going to go down there—"

"No!" Sara held her hand up. "No, you don't. Last time you got involved in my love life, you ended up getting a restraining order against you."

Her friend sat back down. "Yeah, but it was totally

worth it. Besides, I'd never egged a car before. It's a lot harder than you'd think. Some of those little suckers didn't break the first time." She smiled and crossed her legs over themselves, easily folding herself into a little pretzel.

Sara sighed. "It's just…I thought Allen was different. He's the first man that has ever pursued me. You know what I mean? I wasn't looking for a relationship. I had the bakery business to start, my family to deal with. Then there's this whole stalker bit."

Josie sat up a little. "I thought that was over."

Sara shook her head. "I've received a few emails again." She sighed. "I thought for sure it would end when I moved back down here. I was sure it would end, but the emails are coming more frequently now.

"O-M-G! What about the break-in?"

Sara looked at her friend. Her eyes were huge, her face showed shock.

"What do you mean? Do you think the stalker broke in and trashed my place?"

Josie nodded her head.

"No." Sara shook her head. "It doesn't fit his profile. I called Detective Price. He says the stalker would have left one of his calling cards. Like he did when he broke into my apartment."

She shivered inwardly, remembering.

"Well, I'm glad, then." Josie rested her chin on her hands. "Tell me all about this Allen. No, wait." Josie quickly got up and went into their small kitchen. A minute later, she came back with a bottle of wine and two glasses.

"Too bad we don't have any of your cheesecake to go with this." She set the glasses down and started opening the wine.

"There's some in the freezer. You can set it out to thaw and we can have it later."

"Woohoo!" Josie rushed back into the kitchen.

Three hours later, Josie had Sara laughing so hard, she almost forgot all about seeing Allen and the blonde. Almost.

"Then I was like...You can't have a penis-shaped cake for your divorce party made here."

"You did not!" Sara clapped her hands.

"Oh, yes, I did." Josie took another sip of her wine. "Did you know they sell cake pans in penis shapes at the mall? I still have the pan if you want to..." Sara laughed. Yes, having Josie here was just what she needed.

CHAPTER 11

*A*llen stood and knocked on the bakery's back door. He'd tried the front, but when he'd heard the loud music coming from the kitchen, he'd walked around back. Finally, the door flew open, and he was greeted by a short Asian woman with bright blue hair.

"Who are you?" He frowned, trying to look into the back room. The woman's smile dropped to a frown.

"I'm Josie, Sara's new manager, and B-F-F. I know who you are and Sara doesn't want to see you." She started shutting the door in Allen's face. He'd never had to do it his entire life, but for the first time, he stuck his foot in the door and was rewarded with a sharp pain shooting up his foot and leg when Josie slammed the new heavy metal door shut on it.

"Ouch!" He winced at the pain.

"Serves you right for sticking your foot in the door." She stood back and crossed her arms over her chest.

"Why doesn't Sara want to see me?" He pushed the door opened. Josie tried to shut it again.

"Fine, come on in." She waved her hands around. He noticed the front of her apron was covered with flour and she had a smudge of it on her chin.

When he walked into the kitchen, he noticed Sara wasn't there. "Where is she?"

"She's not here." Josie crossed her arms over her chest again.

"Well, why didn't you just say that?" He started walking towards the back door.

"Humph." Josie frowned at him.

"Okay, spill." Allen turned back towards her and mimicked her stance.

"What?"

"Listen, if you are really Sara's B-F-F, then you will tell me why she has been avoiding me the last week."

Josie shook her head. Then she said, "You didn't hear it from me, but if I had caught my boyfriend with a blonde bimbo on his arm, I would have torn said arm from his body." She smiled as he gave her a confused look.

"Blonde bimbo? I haven't been with a blonde bimbo since…Well, never." He unfolded his arms and frowned even more at her. Now her eyebrows shot up and she put her hands on her hips.

"I was there. I saw you walking into the Golden Oar with a tall, skanky looking blonde the day I arrived in town."

Allen thought about it, then he started laughing and didn't stop until Sara rushed in from the other room where she had been hiding with her ear plastered to the door.

"How dare you. How dare you come into my store and laugh at something like that." Her face was flushed, her hair was wild, and she had flour on her apron, in her hair, and on her face. It actually looked like the pair of them had been having a flour war before he'd arrived.

He stopped laughing long enough to smile at her. He walked over and took her shoulders. She tried to pull away, but he held her still. "Were you really jealous?"

"No!" She denied it and shoved his hand off her shoulder. He easily put it back and started pulling her towards him.

"Sure you were. Do you know what it does to me to know that you were jealous? Especially since it was my sister you saw me with." He chuckled again.

"Sister? You said your sister lives in—"

"Maine. She does. She was in California for a business trip and rented a car for the weekend to visit. We tried stopping by the bakery before we went to eat at the restaurant, but you weren't here. I really wish you could have met her." He pulled her closer and held her.

"That was your sister?" Josie asked. He could hear the doubt in her voice. He pulled back and pulled out his cell phone and flipped to an image of Dawn and the kids.

Josie took his phone and smiled, then he handed it to Sara who stared at it for the longest time. He could see a tear slip down her cheek, so he slowly took the phone from her. "You were really that jealous?"

She nodded then shook her head. "I was hurt."

"I'm sorry." He pulled her close, not seeing that Josie had walked out of the kitchen, so they could be alone. "I tried calling you after lunch to see if you were available to meet her. But I guess at that time you were already blocking my calls." He kissed the top of her head as she nodded.

He pulled back and looked into her eyes. How he'd

missed seeing her, holding her. A whole week had gone by and he'd been so busy at work, he hadn't had time to even stop by during lunch. "I'm thinking this"—he waved between them— "is an exclusive deal. I don't mess around if I'm seeing someone, and I hope you feel the same way." She nodded her head and he smiled. "Good. Now that we have our first fight behind us, tell me what that wonderful smell is." She laughed. "I've missed you, but more importantly," he smiled, "I've missed your baking." She laughed harder and punched his shoulder lightly.

"I'd like to see you again, soon. I have an early shift again tomorrow, but I have Saturday off. Maybe we could go on that picnic to Haystack rock?"

She bit her bottom lip. "Hang on." She walked to the door and poked her head out. "Josie? Can you take the interview on Saturday?"

He heard Josie say, "Yes, go for it." Sara laughed and turned back to him, nodding her head.

"Good." He walked towards her. "So, tell me where you found such a bulldog of a best friend."

"I heard that," Josie said from the front room, causing them to laugh.

Saturday rolled around, and Allen drove the winding road with a smile on his face. Sara sat next to him and in the back seat sat a huge basket of homemade sandwiches, soup, and what he could only hope were chocolate chip cookies.

"Did you know that back in the 70s a whale beached itself and died in Florence, just south of here. Well, the small town tried to figure out a way to get rid of the huge, smelling creature, and they decided the best way was to dynamite it."

He looked over at her. "They didn't."

She nodded her head. "Since it had never been done, they didn't know how much dynamite to use and ended up using too much." He chuckled. "There were whale parts for hundreds of miles." He laughed.

"You're making that up." She shook her head.

"Nope." She smiled and looked out the window. "Did you know...?" The rest of the drive up the coast went much like that, funny story after funny story. He didn't know where she got all her history, but some of it was hilarious.

They arrived at Cannon Beach around eleven. A cold breeze was coming in off the water, but the sun was out and there were only a handful of clouds in the sky. Deciding to enjoy the beach first, they took a long stroll up and down the coast. There was a large group of kids flying huge colorful kites, and families walked or ran along the water. Some had even brought their dogs.

"I should have brought Beast." He frowned a little. The dog was getting bigger and had way too much energy for something its size.

Sara smiled. "How is he doing? I bet he's grown."

"Too much. He's become quite the guard dog, though."

"Really?"

"Yeah, someone tried to break in New Year's night. He must have scared them off."

"Well, that's good." Her hair was tied back away from her face, but the wind kept blowing strands around. He stopped her and pulled her closer when they got near the big rock.

"I've missed you." He put his hands on either side of her face and enjoyed the softness of her skin.

"I missed you, too." She wrapped her arms around his neck and rose up to place a soft kiss on his lips. He pulled her closer, not wanting anything between them, not even the breeze.

"I want to be with you, again. Can you stay with me tonight?" He looked down at her, his emotions written clearly in his eyes. He ached for her.

She smiled and nodded. "Josie will take care of the shop until tomorrow afternoon. We open in about a week and there's still so much left to do."

They started walking towards the car to gather their lunch. "You're lucky to have Josie with you." He still hadn't decided what to make of her best friend. He liked the fact that she was protective.

"I was so excited when she said that she'd move down here. I can't imagine running the bakery without her. I wouldn't want to." She smiled and carried the blanket and the thermos of soup while he gathered the large picnic basket.

"Have you hired anyone else?"

She shook her head. "Josie is interviewing two bakers today. One's from Edgeview and the other is a girl I went to school with. To be honest, I'm glad I'm not there. I didn't want to tell her that I just can't stand her." Sara laughed. "I have a few more interviews on Monday, but it's really getting close and I'm starting to get worried."

"You'll find someone." He stopped and looked around. "What about here?"

She looked around and nodded. They were by some pointed rocks that blocked a lot of the wind. Setting the thermos down, she shook out the blanket and straightened it as he set the basket down.

They ate cold sandwiches and warm soup on the beach and lay back to watch the clouds pass by. Then they nibbled on the Death by Chocolate cookies she'd specially made for today.

"I've found a new favorite. These are better than my mother's homemade chocolate cookies." He took his third and bit into the richness. "Death by Chocolate, huh?" He chuckled.

"Yeah, I have a few other great names. There's my favorite, Nut-N-Special. They're these yummy caramel nut bars with chocolate chunks."

He laughed. "How do you come up with everything?" When she looked at him questioningly, he continued. "The names, the recipes, you know...what to make?" She smiled.

"That's the easy part. Most recipes have been handed down to me. Some I've come up with on my own. There are hundreds of recipes out there, you just have to try and find the one that works best."

"Trial and error." He smiled and continued to rub her hair between his fingers. He thought he could just stay there like this all day, but when he felt her shiver, he sat up and they headed back to his truck.

The drive back was a lot quieter than the drive there. Sara seemed to be thinking and he let her. Then she turned to him and asked, "Why the Coast Guard?"

He looked over at her. "Well, when I retired from the SEALs, I knew there were only a handful of things I wanted to do. This was the top of the list."

"Why?"

"I love being a pilot. I love being a teacher even more." He smiled. Yeah, that part he hadn't counted on. "I like molding young minds and bodies into being the best at what we do." He chuckled. "Actually, it's quite funny that I'm enjoying it so much since I gave all my teachers hell when I was younger."

"What boy didn't?" She smiled.

"I remember my first-day teaching. I think I was more nervous than my students. But when I got them in the pool doing drills, I realized that this was where I belonged."

"It's the same for me in the kitchen." She smiled and looked out the window. "Since I was young I would take over cooking dinner, baking. My mother learned early after she found out I was good at it, to just steer clear and let me take over."

"How does she feel about you moving out?"

"Oh, she was sad. Actually, she wondered why Josie didn't just move into the extra bedroom." Sara laughed. "I didn't have the heart to tell her that taking care of them is exhausting. Not that I mind," she quickly put in. "It's just that I need to focus on the bakery right now."

"I know what you mean. It's nice to have family close, but nicer when they don't rely on you so much. When I first got back from Afghanistan, I moved back in with my folks. My father took it as a sign that he no longer had to do anything around the house. I ended up rebuilding the deck and fixing the roof instead of going to my classes."

When they were a few minutes outside of Pride, Sara's phone rang.

"Hello, Josie. How did the interviews go?" Sara's smile fell away. "What?" She listened to her friend then said, "We're five minutes out of town. I'll be there as soon as possible."

When she hung up, she turned to him. He noticed that her face was pale and her hands were shaking.

"Sara?"

"Someone broke into our house." He stepped on the gas a little and decided he could cut the five minutes in half.

CHAPTER 12

*S*ara stood just inside her front door and wanted to cry. Josie's couch and chairs had been cut open and splattered with red paint, much like her furniture had in Seattle. This was her stalker's signature. Her shoulders slumped, and her fingers shook. In Seattle, he had stopped with her items, but this time he had destroyed the house as well. Huge chunks of the drywall were torn out, exposing wires and pipes. The carpet was shredded, leaving places on the floor bare. Even the lights were hanging by the wires.

Allen stepped up behind her and put his hands on her shoulders and she felt a little more centered.

Robert and Larry, his deputy, stood in the mess, taking notes.

"Sara." Robert walked towards her with a frown. "I've already talked to Detective Price. He says he's sending someone down. They want to log everything for their reports."

She nodded. She'd listened to him half-heartedly. Then

Josie walked out of her bedroom, tears streaking down her face. Sara rushed to her and hugged her.

"I'm sorry. I'm so sorry," she mumbled into her friend's hair.

"Ssshhh, it's not your fault." Josie held on tight, then she pulled back and tried to give her a smile. "Now this guy has pissed me off. He better look out."

"It is all my fault." Josie shook her head.

"This creep better run from me now. He stole my favorite sword." Josie's eyes watered a little more. Josie was a collector of swords of any style. Samurai, mid-century, modern. It was a strange hobby for anyone, let alone a five-foot Asian-American baker. But her collection was worth more to her than all of her furniture and other possessions. The knowledge that her stalker had not only ruined everything in their house but had actually stolen a sword turned Sara's stomach.

Larry walked by and coughed. "Sorry, if you have a minute, Miss Cheng, I need to know if there was anything else taken from your room."

Sara watched Josie wipe her face and try to smile. "Sure, I'll be right back." Larry walked into her friend's room and Sara smiled when Josie waved her hand in front of her face and pointed to Larry's back. Josie was right—Larry Buck was tall, blond, and handsome. He always had been, but Sara had known him since they were in diapers together. He was more like the brother she'd never had, but for Josie…She thought of the possibilities.

Allen walked up behind her. "Does Sara need to go through her rooms?"

Robert shook his head. "I'd prefer she stayed clear. At least until the guys get here from Seattle. Maybe you can go into the kitchen, look through everything there." Robert looked at Allen. "If you have a minute?"

"Sure." Allen looked at Sara. "Go ahead, I'll be right in." Sara was too dull to realize that Robert had wanted to talk to Allen alone.

When she entered the kitchen, it reminded her of walking into the bakery last month and her heart skipped a beat. Was her stalker responsible for the mess there as well? Every drawer was opened; every utensil was twisted. Her pans were thrown around, knives stuck out of the walls. Bare wires were hanging from the exposed drywall. Food was thrown on the floor and poured over the countertops. She leaned against the counter and felt like crying. What had she ever done to deserve this? Why was someone so determined to scare and destroy her?

Just like when her apartment had been destroyed, she started running through a list of her ex-boyfriends, ex-coworkers, ex-friends, anyone who would want to do this. No names or faces came to mind. She hadn't realized tears were falling until one fell and landed on her hand, causing her to jump.

Allen walked in just then, a frown on his face. "What do you think about staying with me for a while? Robert doesn't think the place is habitable, at least until the landlord's insurance pays to repair it. He's arranged it so Josie can stay at Amber's apartment since Amber is pretty much living with Luke now. Amber's stuff is still there so it's furnished and everything. Just until we can catch whoever did this."

She shrugged her shoulders.

"If you want, you can stay with Josie?"

"No." She shook her head. "I'll be fine with you for a while. I'd like to stay with you." She tried to smile a little.

A few hours later, they walked into his house. Beast barked and ran in circles to welcome them. When she sat down, and he jumped into her lap, she laughed and smiled. Allen and Robert had packed a few items of hers in a bag, but she didn't want to touch them. Instead, she'd gone over to her mother's house and packed some of her old clothes that she had left there. She'd tossed the other clothes in the trash can.

Josie was all set up at Amber's apartment above Patty's store. She'd worried about her friend, but Josie had insisted. "Besides, it's right across from the bakery. This way I can literally roll out of bed and walk to work." They had taken her to the apartment. Amber had met them and handed over a set of keys.

"I can't thank you enough." Sara had hugged Amber. She'd only known her for a few months but knowing that she was marrying Luke almost made her family.

"I'm never here anymore, anyway." Amber smiled.

"Hey?" Allen said, waking her from her memory. "Do you want something to eat?" She shook her head. "How about some soup?" She shook her head, again. He walked over and sat next to her. "I know you're upset, but you need to eat something."

She looked at him and could see the worry in his eyes. Nodding her head, she said, "Sure. Some soup sounds good."

"Great." She watched him smile and wondered what she'd done to deserve him. "I'll go heat some up." He stood but paused to place a kiss on her head.

She closed her eyes and sighed. She didn't want food.

She felt weary and broken. Not to mention that everything she had was now destroyed, again. She rested her head back against the pillows. Beast curled up beside her and sighed. She rubbed his thick fur and closed her eyes.

Allen looked down at Sara, asleep with Beast curled up beside her. He knew she was probably emotionally tired. He'd been shocked when Robert had pulled him into her bedroom and he'd seen the destruction there.

"Apparently it was much worse in Seattle." Robert flipped his file opened and shook his head. "They sent me her file full of pictures when I was warned about her stalking case."

Allen had looked around her room and felt himself growing mad. Someone had not only destroyed everything she owned but had viciously ripped everything to shreds.

"They used Josie's sword," Robert said behind him. "I haven't told her roommate yet, but he hacked at her bed frame until the sword broke in half." Robert pointed to the corner of the room, where half the sword lay among a pile of Sara's clothes.

Red paint or blood had been splattered over every inch of her room. A large picture of her face had been stapled to her wall and they had hacked at her face until only long shreds remained.

It was obvious to Allen that whoever had done this wanted to hurt Sara, not just scare her. He knew Robert and the Seattle police detective who had shown up felt the same way. Sitting in the chair next to the couch, he picked up the bowl of chili he'd heated up and started eating. Flipping on the TV, he made sure it was muted and watched a basketball game until Sara stirred an hour later. Then he walked in the kitchen and heated her bowl of chili again. By the time he walked back into his living room, she was standing by the back door. Beast was outside running in circles.

"Here." He set the hot bowl on the table. "I have some crackers if you want, instead of the bread."

"No, thank you. This is fine." She walked over and sat down. "Thank you."

He walked over and whistled for Beast, who trotted back into the house.

"Cool trick." She smiled. "Does he know any others?"

Allen laughed. "Not really. I wanted to teach him to sit and beg, but I don't have the patience."

Sara leaned over when Beast ran to her. She broke off a piece of her bread and said sit. The dog surprised him and sat down quickly. "Shake." She picked up the dog's paw and shook it, then set the paw back down and repeated the command. The dog looked at her like she was crazy. She repeated the command and motion a few times before the dog finally got it.

"He's smart," she said as she tossed him a chunk of the bread. "Now see if he remembers it with you."

Beast walked over to him when he called. At first, the dog looked at him like he was crazy when he told him to sit. His doggie eyes went to Allen's hands and when he realized they were empty, he walked back over to Sara. Allen laughed.

"Here, try it with this." She handed him a piece of bread. He repeated it, and this time the dog did everything he asked.

"Now, puppies are ruled by their stomachs. But soon he will want to please you and love will be the reward." She smiled.

"You know a lot about dogs. Have you ever had one?"

She shook her head. "My mother has allergies. I wanted a dog, though, and read up on them one summer. I thought that I could find a way to work around my mother's allergies."

He smiled. "We had an old dog when I was a kid. He didn't know any tricks and farted a lot." She laughed and he smiled. He wanted to make her forget about her stuff. About the mess. She finished her chili and stood to take the bowl to the kitchen.

"Thank you for letting me stay here." She washed the bowl and set it in his dishwasher. He walked up behind her and took her shoulders.

"Sara, I'm letting you stay here because I'm selfish." He smiled. "I want you here, with me. In my kitchen, napping on my couch, sleeping in my bed." His body heated as he pulled her closer and kissed her. He meant to show her tenderness, but when her hands sneaked under his shirt, he felt a piece of his control slip.

"Allen," she moaned under his lips. "Please." She tugged at his shirt until he pulled back and removed it, tossing it across the room. Then his mouth was back on hers as she ran her nails up and down his shoulders and back. She rubbed her body next to his until he pulled her up, letting her sit on the countertop. She wrapped her legs around his hips and he rubbed himself against her jeans, enjoying the friction until he had to have her naked. His hands pushed at her sweater until he pushed it up and over her head, exposing her bra. He stood back and enjoyed the view. Her red lacy bra begged for his attention. He dipped his head and ran his mouth over the soft material. Her head dropped back and she moaned as she ran her fingers in his hair, pulling him closer.

Then she was reaching for his jeans. He was breathless and felt the last shred of his control snap when she leaned back on the countertop and her marvelous breasts were finally exposed. He pulled at her jeans until she helped him remove them, while she still balanced on the marble countertop. Her red panties matched her top and he dipped his head to taste them and to taste her. Her breath hitched and she let out a groan when he dipped his finger under the lace and felt her silky skin. He hitched her legs over his shoulders, exposing her even further to his torture. Pulling her panties aside, he touched his mouth to her and had her squirming and moaning. Then, when he thought he couldn't control himself anymore, he yanked his pants down, sheathed himself, and slid into her, slowly. Twin moans echoed in the large room.

She was leaning back on his countertop so that her elbows were resting on the back of his bar area. The soft lighting and the sweet motion of their movement was almost his undoing. Finally, he felt her convulse under him and let himself go.

It didn't take him long to realize they need to move. His socks kept slipping on the tile floor, so he pulled her up and carried her upstairs and set her gently on the bed. Her eyes were closed, and her breathing was shallow. He didn't know if she was sleeping or if she was still recovering. He stood over her and looked down at her. She was beautiful. Her long curly hair splayed out over his bedspread. Her skin was glowing from the day in the sun and from the heated sex.

"What?" She opened one eye and smiled.

"Just looking." He ran his eyes over her and smiled. "I'm allowed to do that, I think."

"Yes. You are." She smiled up at him. "As long as it's me you're looking at."

He crawled onto the mattress and wrapped his arms around her. "Honey, there's no one else I'd rather be looking at than you. You're beautiful." He placed a kiss on her neck then traveled his mouth up to her ear where he whispered, "I love looking at you after I've made you come. Your skin glows."

"Oh, God!" She wrapped her legs around him and held on.

"Your hair is a mess from my hands, your lips are pink and swollen from mine." He kissed her mouth, lingering there for a moment. He felt her hips starting to move against his hips and slid slowly into her.

"Oh, Allen." She closed her eyes and rolled her head back for him to rain kisses along her skin. He enjoyed every inch of her, taking his time this time, spending minutes on every inch of her until he felt her tighten around him. Then he started it all over again until finally, much later, he joined her again and fell asleep holding her, his face buried in her hair, a smile on her lips.

CHAPTER 13

Sara woke to barking and for a moment was disoriented.

"Quiet. You'll wake Sara."

"Too late." She smiled and stretched her arms over her head. It had been a week since the break-in at the house. Today was the grand opening for Sara's Nook. Rolling over, she looked at the alarm and almost shot out of bed.

"It's four o'clock. How can it be four o'clock?" She pushed out of bed and forced herself to take a deep breath in, then out. Stress was not her friend. Not on opening day.

"You said you wanted to be woken at four. It's five til. You still have five minutes." Allen frowned at her as he opened the door for Beast to come in. The dog rushed in, ran in circles and barked.

"He needs to go out."

"Yeah, hang on buddy. I've gotta put some boots on. It's snowing out there." Allen stepped into his other boot. He was wearing the bottoms of flannel pajamas. No shirt. She sighed and wished she could spend the whole day exploring that chest. But when he strolled out the door, the dog closely following, the alarm went off and she jumped from the bed to hit the shower.

When she walked into the bakery, Josie was there already rolling out the dough for the sweet bread.

Josie stopped what she was doing and rushed over to her. "Opening day!" They jumped up and down laughing. Rosalyn, the other baker they had hired just two days ago, stood in the corner smiling. Sara didn't know the woman very well since she'd moved here from Seaside, but her resume was impressive, and she knew her way around the kitchen.

"Okay," Sara sobered, "enough of that." Josie followed her lead.

"Yes." She cleared her throat. Then the two of them were jumping up and down laughing and singing, "Opening day" again.

An hour before opening, Sara felt all the nerves bubbling up. Becca arrived in her uniform, a Sara's Nook t-shirt, which had come in the mail yesterday, and black jeans. Her sister looked good and Sara knew she would do her best to present the bakery in the best light. Even though she could only work weekends, Becca looked forward to helping out as much as she could.

They still were looking for someone part-time to cover the front during the day. Until then, Sara or Josie would have to fill in.

Fifteen minutes before they would open the doors, she looked out front and was shocked to see a line growing outside. Even in the cold, people were lined up around the street corner.

The place smelled great and the food looked even

better. They were just putting on the finishing touches when she signaled Becca to open the doors.

Four hours later, Sara sat down and closed her eyes, a huge smile on her face. "I'd say that was a successful opening."

There had been a steady stream of people for the first two hours. After that, people came and went. Some people ordered and took it to go on their way to work, others ordered and ate in, filling the place so that, at times, the only room was standing room. People utilized the bar area she'd had the Timothy's build along the window wall. They had run out of blueberry muffins and Death by Chocolate cupcakes, and they'd had to quickly rush and make more.

"The lull before lunch." Josie sat down next to her. They sat at a high-top table, watching Becca clear the rest of the tables.

"I think everyone from town came in this morning." Becca smiled.

"Yes, and no one could get over how wonderful of a job you'd done." Josie smiled.

"Lunch should be slower." She nibbled on her lip. She knew that the Golden Oar would always be there, but her sandwiches and soup were great for people who had to have a quick lunch and didn't have time for a sit-down meal. They even offered paper bag lunches, ready for those in a real hurry. It was the closest thing to a drive-through that Pride had or would ever see.

They had almost two dozen special orders that would need to be filled. She had Rosalyn working on some of them already. Every item on her menu had been ordered, but by far the coffee and lattes had been the biggest hit.

Almost everyone who entered her door had walked out with a decorative Sara's Nook thermal coffee mug, which could be refilled at a fraction of the cost, rather than purchasing a coffee in a paper cup.

A half an hour later, the lunch crowd started coming in and by the time Sara closed the front doors at two, her feet hurt. They still had a few hours of baking to do for special orders that would be picked up tomorrow, and some prep work that needed to be done, but she was looking forward to a quiet night at Allen's. When Josie asked if she wanted to come over to the apartment and celebrate the success of the day, she wavered. But seeing her friend's face, she decided to enjoy the night with her friend and text Allen her plans to stay late.

Since she'd driven her own car today, which was already parked across the street, she could drive herself back to his place later.

When they closed up the store an hour later, they walked arm in arm across the street.

"I have a bottle of champagne I bought just for this occasion," Josie said as she started skipping.

"Champagne? What would we have done had the day not been so successful?" Sara asked.

"Drank away our worries." They both laughed.

When they walked up the stairs to the apartment above O'Neil's store, Sara realized how tired she was, but she didn't want to let her friend down. One glass, she told herself.

One and a half glasses and a large piece of brownie later, she waved at Josie as she backed out of the parking lot. It was just past nine and she noticed Patty had already closed up shop. Patty's closed early on the weekends, but

Sara's eyes were on the bakery. The windows were dark and the sign that hung over the windows shown with brightness. "Sara's Nook" sat in fancy print with "Bakery, Deli, Catering" below in simple fonts. She'd never been prouder of anything in her life.

Allen had called her and told her he had taken someone else's shift for the night and wouldn't be home until late. She had considered staying at Josie's, but then she thought of Beast. The poor dog probably needed to go out.

When she drove up to the house, she heard him scratching at the door. "I'm coming, boy." She grabbed her bag and hurried towards the door. The rain was just starting, and she almost slipped on the stone pathway that led to the mudroom door. She was digging in her purse, looking for the keys that Allen had given her when the world went dark.

Allen drove up his driveway and smiled when he saw Sara's car parked in front of the garage. He'd stopped by for breakfast and lunch today and knew the place had been packed both times. He hadn't gotten to see her for the breakfast rush because it had been too busy, but he'd pulled her aside at lunch and had kissed her until he'd felt her vibrating. He couldn't wait to do it again.

When he parked his truck, the lights reflected on something on the stone path. He rushed out of the truck, leaving it running.

"Sara!" he screamed over and over again as he pulled her into his arms. She was cold, very cold. He noticed the blood on the stone and the ground below her. His hands shook as he felt her neck for a pulse. When he felt a weak one, he quickly pulled his cell phone from his pocket and dialed 911.

Later, he stood in the emergency room at Edgeview hospital when Patricia Lander rushed, Becca on her heels. "Where is she?"

"They've got her in x-ray," Allen said, pushing his hair away from his forehead. It was taking too long. It had been at least fifteen minutes since they'd rolled her to the back. He'd called her mother five minutes after they'd arrived at the hospital via ambulance. He'd followed them the entire time, silently praying that she'd be okay.

He hadn't even stopped to let Beast out but had left that to Robert, who'd shown up before the ambulance.

"She must have slipped," he'd told him. Robert had looked at the situation and frowned. Allen didn't like what he knew that meant. Robert had asked to look around after he'd covered Sara up with a thermal blanket and made sure Allen didn't try to move her. Allen had tossed him the house keys and told him to do whatever he wanted.

Just then the doctor came out. "Mrs. Lander." He walked up to her and nodded his head. "Becca. Why don't we go to my office?" He started walking down the hall.

"Please, can Allen come along?" Becca turned and took his arm. The doctor frowned.

"Yes, he's with Sara. He was the one who found her." Patricia took his other arm.

"I'll leave it up to you." The doctor continued on his way, with the three of them following.

When everyone was crammed into the small office, the doctor behind his desk, he sat back and frowned.

"Sara has a concussion and a nasty cut on the back of

her head. Now, this could have happened by either a fall, as suggested by Mr. Masters here, or she could have been attacked. What makes me lean towards the latter is the large chunk of wood we found lodged in her skin. You told the officer on scene that she was found on your stone pathway and that there was nothing near her."

"Yes," Allen frowned. "There aren't any trees or bushes around that pathway. There weren't any logs or branches near where I found her. It looked, at least to me, like she had slipped on the stones and fallen back. But...if she was hit over the head with something..." He stood and took two steps. "I need to call Robert."

"I've already notified him. He told me he'll be here shortly. All we can do is wait. Sara hasn't woken up yet and we are watching her closely."

"Thank you, Eugene." Patricia smiled at the man. The doctor took her hand in his and smiled back at her.

"If there's anything more I can do, just let me know." He patted her hand and then walked over and opened his door.

When they walked out, Josie came rushing towards them. "Where is she? Is she okay?" Deputy Larry was right behind her.

"She's resting." The doctor looked at Josie, then he turned to Allen and said, "You can see her one at a time. Follow me, I'll show you to her room."

When Larry followed along, Becca looked at Josie with questions in her eyes. She shrugged her shoulders.

"I'd had three glasses of champagne, so I called the station and Larry drove me up here." Becca waved towards him. Larry followed them upstairs, where they took turns seeing Sara. Everyone agreed to allow Allen to stay with her the longest.

Robert showed up soon after and when Allen walked out of Sara's room to give Josie her turn, he pulled Robert aside and bombarded him with questions.

"Hang on, hang on. I've got a million of the same questions that you do. No, I didn't find anything that she could have hit her head on other than the stones and grass. I did find a huge tree branch a few yards away, but at this point, I can't be sure if it's what was used. I did find tire tracks in the mud down the road. It looks like a car pulled off just above your place, did a U-turn, and parked. No footprints, though. We've taken molds, but the chances…"

"Yeah." Allen started pacing in front of Robert. He wanted action. He wanted to rip someone apart. But he had to know that Sara was okay first.

"I took care of your dog. He's at our place until you can make it back."

"Thanks."

"Hey, don't thank me. Now that my kids have a puppy to play with, my next stop for the day is to see if Marcus has any more. Even Amelia is behind it." He shook his head. "How's she doing?"

Allen relayed what the doctor had told them an hour earlier.

"Anything missing at the place?"

"No, it doesn't appear they entered your place. I drove by the bakery just to make sure. The alarm is still on and everything looked clear, but we'll be keeping an eye on it more closely."

"Thanks." Allen was focusing on the door to Sara's room. When Josie walked out, tears streaming down her face, he wanted to go over and comfort her, but instead, she walked into Larry's waiting arms. Both Robert and Allen noticed the move. Larry looked away with a slight smile on his lips.

Sara's mother and sister took turns next, and by two in the morning, Allen settled down in the chair next to Sara's bed.

CHAPTER 14

*A*round seven the next morning, Sara woke to find Allen stretched out on a small chair, his head rolled all the way back, resting on the wall. When she tried to move, pain shot from the back of her skull down her shoulders and arms.

Gripping her head, she moved slowly until finally, she sat up. She must have made a lot of noise because Allen was by her side when she opened her eyes again.

"How are you feeling?" He had dark circles under his eyes and his clothes were wrinkled.

"My head hurts. Did I slip on the rocks?" He shook his head.

"What do you remember?" He took her hand and held it in his.

She closed her eyes and thought about it. "I was walking towards the mudroom door. Beast was whining and scratching at the door to be let out. I remember the stones were slippery." She tilted her head, the slight motion sending pain shooting through her neck. Closing her eyes on the pain, she said, "That's it."

"The doctor and Robert think that you were attacked."

Sara's eyes flew open. "My stalker?"

"They don't know. What time did you get home?"

She closed her eyes again. She was finding the darkness soothing. "I left Josie's around ten."

"I drove up at a quarter to eleven. Does the light bother you?" She heard him stand up and walk away, not wanting to chance to open her eyes again until he said. "I've turned the lights off. See if that helps." When she opened them again, he was standing beside her.

"It does. Thank you. Are my mother and sister here?"

"I'm not sure. Let me go check." He walked to the door. Five minutes later, her mother and sister walked in. A few minutes later, the doctor and nurses walked in and pushed everyone out of the room.

A concussion hurt a lot more than she would have thought. When she moved too much, her stomach threatened to revolt so she lay as still as she could. Turning her head hurt her neck and back, so she didn't. They ended up keeping her for one more night. Josie showed up later that evening.

"Don't worry. Everything went smoothly today. Allen called and kept me up to date on your status. Otherwise, I wouldn't have made it through the day." Josie held her hand. "I should have forced you to stay the night."

"No, it's not your fault. Like you've told me a million times, there was nothing we could have done."

"You're right. I know it." Her friend pulled out a box. "I brought you some of my rice crispy treats. I know how you love them."

Sara smiled. "The ones with the chocolate chips and caramel in them?"

Josie smiled. "Of course."

The next day Sara sat up on Allen's couch, surrounded by a dozen people. It was a tradition in Pride, something she'd always grown up with, that when someone was in need, the whole town gathered behind them.

There was more food than people and the noise level was almost causing her head to explode, but she smiled and talked to everyone, enjoying the support.

Allen, for the most part, stood in the corner frowning. His buddies were right there with him. She was sure they were all trying to come up with a plan of attack. But how did you attack someone when you had no clue who it was?"

"They are probably working out a schedule," Allison said beside her.

"Schedule?" Beast was snuggled on her lap, causing her to be warm.

"Sure. Remember what they did for me when Kevin was stalking me? They never left me alone for a moment. It was quite annoying, and also very thoughtful." Allison smiled.

"Oh, yeah." Sara looked off towards the men and realized her friend was right. They were all looking down at their phones, most likely scheduling their shifts.

After everyone left, Sara lay down on the couch while Allen finished cleaning up. She must have fallen asleep because she woke to him carrying her upstairs.

"I guess I'm a little tired."

"Yeah, it's been a busy day. Do you want anything?"

"No." She snuggled into his chest and sighed. "Just you."

When he reached the room, he laid her down on the bed and removed her shoes, then he pulled off his shirt and crawled in next to her. She tried to pull him closer for a kiss, but he looked down at her. "You need your rest. There will be time for us later after you feel better."

"Hmm," She snuggled into his arms and fell asleep to the sound of his heartbeat.

Over the course of the next few days, she wasn't left alone. Allen finally let her go back into the bakery on Tuesday. He dropped her off and picked her up. When he worked late, Josie or Allison stayed with her at the house. When they were unavailable, Todd, Iian, or Robert were there.

She didn't mind it, really. But a week later, she was starting to wonder how much longer everyone could continue living like this.

Allen was on his hundredth lap when he looked up through the water and saw Robert standing at the edge of the pool. Pulling himself out, he took his towel and started drying off.

"We might have a break." Robert handed him a folder.

Opening the file, Allen read the report as Robert talked to him.

"It appears that Stephan and Bethany Mathis, Sara's old bosses at Seattle's West Bakery, are getting a divorce. Mrs. Mathis has accused her husband of being unfaithful with one of their employees. No names were listed, but when I started checking into things, I called and asked Mr. Mathis his whereabouts at the time of Sara's attack. He gave me an alibi that didn't check out. Looking into it further, I found a car he'd rented with his credit card. The mileage and return date check out with a trip down here. I told the detectives in Seattle, and they brought him in for further questioning."

"Do you think Sara and…" He couldn't say it.

Robert shook his head. "No, in her file she stated she hadn't been in any relationships with him."

He felt his breath leave his chest in relief. He should have never thought that she would get involved with a married man, let alone her boss.

"In questioning, he claims he was home alone that night. Said it was the day his wife served him with divorce papers. Apparently, the business is in her name and he stands to lose quite a bit if she can prove he's been cheating on her."

"If Sara and he…" He couldn't bring himself to say it. "If Sara had nothing to do with him, why would he be after her?"

"Why does any man stalk a woman? Sick in the head, if you ask me." Robert shook his head. "Anyway, I thought I ought to let you know before I go to Sara with this information."

"Let me," Allen piped in. "She might take it better."

"Are you sure?"

"Yeah, I'm picking her up"—he looked at his watch— "in half an hour anyway."

"Okay. If there's anything else, you need."

"Do they have enough to keep him?"

Robert shook his head. "Not at this time. I'll let you know if they find anything else."

"Thanks." Allen shook his hand and went to get dressed so he could pick Sara up at the bakery.

When he got to the bakery, he was shocked at the transformation. Red and pink hearts were everywhere. Most of the cookies in the front refrigerators were now covered in pink, red, and white frosting. Even the cakes and cupcakes were decorated as such.

At first, his mind refused to connect, then he saw a sign with Valentine Specials written on it. Valentine's? It was only…He looked at his watch for the date. February first.

He supposed people started thinking that far ahead for events like this, but he wasn't one of them.

The bakery was packed with people. Checking his watch again, he noticed he was five minutes early. When he walked into the back room, she was rushing around.

"Hey," he called out and sat on a stool and nibbled on the cookie Becca had given him as he walked by the front.

"Hey." She turned and looked at him, pushing a strand of hair out of her eyes. "You're early." She looked at the clock. "Where did the time go?" She said this with a smile. He couldn't image why she liked working in a hot kitchen all day. He'd rather have his nails pulled out one at a time. Slowly. But he did enjoy the perks. The hot cookie melted in his mouth and sent something close to a shiver up his spine.

"What are these called?" Sara looked over at him as he waved the chocolate cookie around.

"Chocolate melts. Do you like them?"

"Best cookie…ever." He smiled when she laughed.

"I'm almost done here."

"That's okay. I thought we'd head to the Golden Oar for dinner."

"Sounds wonderful. I'm ready for someone else to cook for me." She dusted off her hands.

"Larry's taking me there tomorrow night," Josie said, smiling from across the room.

"How's that going?" Allen leaned on the wall and crossed his arms. He didn't know Larry all that well, but he knew he and Sara had been lifelong friends.

"Great." Josie beamed. "Just wonderful."

"You can't tell, because she's so short," Sara laughed, "but she's been floating around here all day. I say it's love."

Josie smiled at her. "I'd say I'm not the only one feeling those effects, either." Josie pointed to her and Allen almost choked on his bite of cookie.

Sara looked over at him with concern in her eyes. She'd probably gotten the wrong idea and had thought that it had freaked him out, the thought of her falling for him, but it had actually been the opposite. Ever since the attack, he'd been trying to work up the nerve to tell her how he felt about her. He'd never fallen before, so it had come as a shock to him that it had happened so quickly.

He'd been planning on making it a special event, but he just didn't know how yet.

When they drove to the restaurant in silence, she stopped him before he could get out of the truck.

"Josie was just joking."

"Hmm?" He turned to look at her. Her curly hair was tied up in a loose braid, tiny wisps hung around her face. He leaned over and placed a kiss on her lips. "I know. I think I'm finally getting her humor." He smiled as he

161

pulled away. "Besides, you should be the one to tell me you love me." He gave her his wickedest smile. "After all, it's hard to resist this." He waved his hand up and down in front of himself.

She laughed, getting his joke. "Yes, what woman could resist your charms?"

"Certainly not you." He leaned over and kissed her again. "I know I have a hard time resisting your...baking." He quickly ducked her light punch and got out of the truck to walk around and open the door for her. Helping her down, he pulled her into his arms and kissed her until they were both breathless. "Maybe we should grab dinner to go?" He ran his mouth down the column of her neck, enjoying the smell and taste of her. "Sugar. How is it you taste like sugar?"

She laughed. "Josie throws it at me." She giggled when he ran his tongue over her neck.

"Mmmm, better than those melted cookies." She laughed.

"Chocolate Melts."

"Yeah."

Just then they heard a cough and looked over to see Iian and Allison standing there smiling at them. Conner was tugging on Allison's hand until she finally let him go. He ran right into Sara's arms. She picked him up effort-lessly and twirled him around as the little boy squealed with delight.

"We were just coming in for some dinner," Allen said.

Allison signed as she spoke. "So were we. Conner and I were, at least. Iian was just meeting us outside."

"What do you say to grabbing a big table together?" Sara looked at him. How could he deny her? He'd wanted to tell her the news he'd learned from Robert, but he knew they had plenty of time that night.

"Sounds like a plan."

It was nice having friends to laugh and joke with over dinner. It was normally hard to communicate with Iian since he rarely liked to speak, but with Allison there as an interpreter, the night went smoothly.

"You know, we were wondering if you'd be interested in offering some desserts here," Allison said once everyone's plates were empty. "We have our standard desserts, but they just don't compare." Allison smiled.

"Sure, I bet we can work something out." He could see the spark in Sara's eyes with the possibilities.

"Wonderful," Iian said. "I tried your white chocolate cheesecake the other day." Iian rolled his eyes. "Best I've ever had."

"Thank you." Allen watched Sara blush a little.

"Have you heard anything about the attack?" Allison asked, holding her sleeping son against her growing belly.

Sara shook her head and looked down at her hands.

Allen grabbed her hand. "Actually, Robert came to see me right before I drove over." He spent the next few minutes relaying what Robert had told him.

"I just can't believe Mr. Mathis is behind all this." She chewed her bottom lip. "Sure, he was a pain and always hitting on his employees, but to do everything..." He watched her shiver. "I just don't see it." Her face dropped a little. "Poor Bethany. What is she going through? She was a tough boss, but she didn't deserve this."

"People can be sick," Allison said. "When Kevin Williams burned down my house with my mother inside, no one in town would have thought he could have done something like that. But he'd changed. Maybe your Mr. Mathis is going through some rough times."

Sara looked out the large windows towards the choppy waters, deep in thought. "I suppose."

"I'm just thankful they finally have a lead. The rental car, his lack of alibi," Allen said. "Maybe now we can all get back to our normal lives and Sara can be safe."

CHAPTER 15

The next day Robert came around and told Sara that there had been enough cause to book Stephan Mathis. The tire treads matched the molds taken by the house, the rental car company confirmed that the car had been rented with his credit card, and Stephan didn't have solid alibis for any of the events. Even the night her Seattle apartment had been vandalized, his only alibi was he'd been at home watching sports and drinking beer alone.

Sara felt like a weight had lifted off her chest. She hadn't realized that for the last four years she'd been living in terror. Finally, she could go where she wanted without fear.

Besides, one of her favorite times of the year was right around the corner, and this year she had reason to celebrate it. Valentine's Day had always been high on her list, along with playing dress up during Halloween. She'd celebrated plenty of Valentine's Days with boyfriends, but this was the first she'd celebrate knowing she was truly in love. She enjoyed decorating the bakery and enjoyed cooking the specialty items for the season even more. Now all she had to do was tell Allen how she felt, and she knew exactly how she was going to do it. She'd been sketching up her plans all week since they'd hung all the Valentine's decorations.

Josie had signed the lease on the apartment above Patty's place. Since the house they'd rented was still being renovated, the landlady had canceled the lease. She'd even refunded them their whole deposit. Sara hadn't really given much thought to staying longer at Allen's. She still questioned what he really felt about it, but every time she asked, he'd tell her that he loved having her there.

They'd gone shopping in Edgeview for new clothes and toiletry items since she'd been running low on everything. She'd gone shopping with Josie on another day and brought Allen a special Valentine's gift. She kept the see-through black-and-pink teddy hidden until the right moment. She'd even bought a special dress for the occasion she had planned.

She knew the days before a major holiday were going to be busy, but she didn't know that it would be crazy busy. She and Josie ended up staying past eleven most nights working on special orders and the orders for the Golden Oar.

She knew she had to hire another full-time baker but decided to hold off interviewing until things slowed down.

Since Allen had moved his shifts around during the time they'd been unclear who was stalking her, he found himself working doubles to catch up. Most nights she arrived home an hour or two before he did. Some mornings he was gone before she even woke up.

They'd fallen into a pattern, spending their days off together, even if it meant he sat down at the bakery for a few hours watching her work.

This weekend though, she had their special dinner planned and she wasn't going to let anything get in the way of her plans.

She spent the night before their date working at the bakery alone. She wanted everything just perfect. When there was a knock on the back door, she almost jumped. Looking out the peephole, she was shocked to see Bethany Mathis standing in the rain.

Sara disarmed the security system and opened the door a little. "Bethany? What are you doing here?"

Bethany had been Sara's boss for the four years she'd worked in Seattle. She was a larger woman who hadn't given her appearance much attention. She'd spent most of her time in the kitchen, baking. Something Sara had forced herself to learn from Bethany was to always maintain a life outside of the kitchen. Smiling a little, she opened the door farther. The larger woman's face was red and Sara could tell that she'd been crying.

"I'm sorry to bother you. I tried to make it here earlier before you closed, but something came up at the shop."

"Please," Sara motioned for her to come in. Whatever the pain the woman's husband had caused her, Sara couldn't say much against Bethany. The woman had been a wonderful boss, caring and kind the entire time she'd worked for her. "Can I get you anything?"

"No, thank you." Bethany took a tissue out of her pocket and wiped at her nose. "I've been meaning to get down here and see your place." She looked around, walking farther into the kitchen.

Sara shut the door behind her. She didn't know what to say to the woman whose husband had caused her so much grief.

"You've really made a place for yourself here," Bethany said, her back to Sara. "I suppose I should have seen this coming."

Sara stood still, unsure of what she'd just heard. Then Bethany turned around, a smile pasted on her lips. "Stephan was always talking about how talented you were. Sara this. Sara that. It drove me nuts!" She screamed the last part.

"I'm sorry. I know you must be upset." Sara tried to think how she'd feel if her husband had been cheating on her and stalking one of her employees.

"Upset? Upset!" Bethany laughed. "You think I'm upset?" She crossed her arms over her chest and started walking around, running her hands over the tables and utensils. "I'm more than upset. When I found out how Stephan felt about you, I knew he'd cheated before. I always looked the other way, but with you, it was different. He couldn't stop talking about you. Every time you walked into the room, I saw it there in his eyes." She turned and glared at her. "Love." The word sounded like poison coming from her lips. "So, I decided to take matters into my own hands."

Sara's back was to the door, but she was so frozen in place, she didn't think she could blink, let alone breathe. Bethany's fingers ran over the row of knives hanging on the magnet.

"Breaking into your apartment was easy and fun." She smiled, and Sara gasped. "Oh yes, cutting up your things gave me great pleasure. Everything you are is tainted."

Sara gripped behind her, looking for the door handle. "Then you gave your notice and left. I thought things would change. I thought Stephan would finally pay attention to me again, but he didn't. Instead, he would go away for days at a time. I knew he was coming down here to you." She screamed, and slowly slid the largest knife off the wall magnet. The metal on metal sound echoed in the empty building.

"I'd been coming down here, trying to catch the two of you together, but you were too sneaky for me. I followed you everywhere you went. Everywhere! Then it became clear to me. I needed to get rid of you once and for all. I thought the hit over the head would work, but I guess I didn't hit you hard enough."

"But aren't you divorcing him?"

"Of course!" Bethany started walking slowly towards her. She dragged the sharp knife along the top of the worktable, leaving behind a large scratch. "I had to keep up my appearances." She stopped a few feet from her, smiling. Sara could see it now, the empty look that showed the evil inside. "I handed him the papers, then I drove down here on his credit card and hit you over the head with the largest stick I could find. I wanted to kill you. I will kill you. It will be easier after you're gone. Stephan will be cleared, then he'll come running back to me like he always does. And you won't be around to distract him."

Bethany lunged, the knife held high. Sara saw the lights sparkle off the sharp edge just before she screamed.

Allen smiled and looked down at Beast. He'd spent the last

hour bathing him. The dog now smelled as good as he looked. Frowning, Allen looked down at himself and then looked at the clock. He had just enough time for a quick shower before his plans. He'd kept his secret from Sara all week and it was killing him.

Jogging upstairs, he looked over his shoulder. "Don't go messing anything up, buddy. We've got a date tonight."

He knew it was early, that Valentine's Day wasn't until this weekend, but he had overheard Sara telling Josie that they'd be too busy that day to do anything other than work. So he'd decided an early Valentine couldn't hurt. Plus, she wouldn't be expecting it.

After showering, he put on his new jeans and shirt and took a look at his reflection. Yup, he was ready for this, he told himself.

It took some doing getting Beast and the large box into the truck. He finally decided to put the box in first and then go back for the dog. Beast now weighed almost a hundred pounds, easily.

Driving through town, he smiled as he stopped in front of the bakery. She'd sure outdone herself with the window decorations. The pink, red, and white lights flashed in the window. She'd even changed the blubs in her sign so that her lettering showed up with a slight tint of pink.

Yeah, love was in the air. He opened the door for Beast to jump out. It was raining lightly, and he frowned at the sky. "Looks like we're going to get a little wet." Couldn't the weather work with him for one night? Hoping it would clear by the time they made it to the beach, he walked to the back bakery door just as Sara pushed out of it, screaming. She ran right into his arms, yelling, "She has a knife!"

For a split second, he thought she and Josie were just

fooling around, but then a large woman with bright blonde hair came rushing out the door, waving a large knife. In a blink of an eye, Beast had his jaws wrapped around the woman's wrist, the one with the knife in it. The woman screamed and dropped the knife and tried to kick the dog off of her.

"Dial 911." Allen shoved his cell phone into Sara's hands, then he walked over and kicked the knife away from the woman before pulling Beast back two steps. Allen told him to sit and he did, but he didn't stop growling and glaring at the woman.

"Who are you?" Allen asked, hearing Sara talking on the phone behind him.

"That dog attacked me. I'm going to sue."

"Who are you?" he demanded a little louder.

"I'm Bethany Mathis, and that dog attacked me on her property." She pointed to Sara. "I was just walking out the door, minding my own business when he attacked me. Look at my wrist. I think he broke it!" she screeched.

Allen saw the red marks on the woman's wrist. Beast had broken skin, but there was no way he'd broken her wrist.

"I'm leaving. I'm going to go call my lawyer."

"You'll stay right where you are." Beast's growling became louder when the woman started to move. "We'll just wait and see what Robert says when he arrives."

"I don't care what you say. I'm leaving. If that dog attacks me again, I'll have him shot." She smiled, and Allen could see the wickedness in her face.

"They're coming," Sara said, standing behind him. He felt her shiver and wanted to tell her to go inside, but he knew she wouldn't leave him. Didn't want to leave him.

"Hold Beast," he said softly.

Sara bent down and knelt next to her protector. When she started to rub between his ears, his growling stopped. "Thank you," he heard her whisper into his ear. He smiled when he heard the sirens in front of the building.

"What's going on?" Robert said when he stepped out of his patrol car.

An hour later, Sara and Allen sat in the bakery's dining room. Beast lay by their feet. He'd lit some candles and placed them all around the room. They sat there alone, eating the picnic he'd packed for their romantic dinner on the beach. The steady rain pelted down outside. Robert had hauled Bethany Mathis away after her confession to Sara had been retold. The woman had denied it up until the point that Robert put her into the back of the patrol car. Then she'd screamed, "I'll kill you yet, you bitch," sealing her fate.

Allen looked across the small table at Sara. Gone was the weary, scared look he'd seen an hour earlier. Now her eyes sparkled, and he could tell she was really enjoying their dinner. "I'm sorry the night didn't turn out exactly as I planned." He looked across at her and took her hand.

"It's perfect." She smiled and nibbled on her roll. He'd cooked lasagna, one of her favorites. He'd gotten the recipe from her mother and had spent three hours cooking it today. He'd burned the first one, but he'd had enough time and ingredients to try it again. This time it had turned out perfect.

"I really wanted to do this at the beach. That's where I imagined it all."

"What?" She took a sip of her wine and set the glass down when he reached for her hand.

"Sara, I know we've only known each other for a few months, but I feel like I've known you..." He cleared his throat and stood up. "This isn't going like I planned." He turned to her and tried to smile. She sat there and looked up at him. "Listen, I can't think when I'm around you. I had everything planned out, but seeing you in the candlelight, it does something to me." He stood over her and became more frustrated that he didn't have the right words. "My tongue gets tied, my palms sweat. I don't know what I would have done if anything had happened to you. I almost lost you once and I don't think I could bear it if it happened again." He knelt next to her. "Sara, I'm trying to tell you that I love you."

She smiled and took his face in her hands. "I love you, too, Allen." She laid her lips on his and he released the breath he'd been holding.

CHAPTER 16

*E*verything had turned out perfectly, she thought, as she looked up at Allen. He may think he didn't have the right words, but what he had said meant more to her than any poem.

The soft candlelight, the romantic dinner here at her bakery. When he pulled her up to stand next to him, she pulled away for a moment.

"I have something for you. It's a two-part gift, but I don't see why you can't enjoy the first part tonight." She started walking backward. "Stay right here. I'll be right back." She rushed into the kitchen and pulled out the masterpiece that she'd finished minutes before Bethany had shown up.

Pushing the door open with her back, she turned and presented her gift. His eyes went huge and he started laughing when he saw it.

Therein vanilla and chocolate were his and Beast's faces with the words "I Love You Both" written below.

He walked forwards and took the cake from her.

"Wow! Look at this." He moved it closer to the candles to get a better look. "How did you do this?" He set the cake down and looked at it.

"Practice." She smiled and stood next to him.

"It's perfect. I can't believe it. I've never seen anything like this before." He reached into his pocket and snapped a picture with his phone. "I've got to send this to someone. I mean, there ought to be an award." He smiled down at her.

"Well, it was easy. The two of you are such easy models."

He laughed. "Right." He turned to her and pulled her closer, placing a kiss on her lips. She held him close, not letting him pull away.

"Mmm, more." She wrapped her arms around his shoulders as he deepened the kiss. Then he started walking her backward, towards the kitchen.

"Allen," she laughed, "where are we going?"

"Kitchen. There are too many windows here. Too many people that might walk by," he said against her lips.

"Really?" She laughed when he pulled her into the kitchen and pushed her against the wall, his hands running over every inch of her.

"I have to have you. I love you, so much." He repeated it over and over as he rained kisses over every inch of her. She'd never stood naked in her kitchen before, never imagined she'd be doing so, but now they were both naked and out of breath. Just before she crested, she brought her mouth to his ear and whispered, "I love you, Allen."

The next morning the bakery was crowded. Everyone had

heard what had happened the night before. Some came hoping to hear the details, some came just to have a warm breakfast. But almost everyone in town stopped by.

Her Valentine's baskets had been such a huge hit that she'd run out and had had to purchase small baskets at the local hardware store to replace the ones she'd special ordered.

Halfway through the day, Zach showed up. He shuffled his feet, looking down, and apologized for New Year's. She hadn't seen him since that night and asked him where he'd been.

"AA." He looked embarrassed. "After New Year's, I decided it was about time I got some help. I overheard at the Golden Oar what happened here last night, and I just wanted to stop by and make sure everything was alright."

"Yes, thank you. I'm so glad you did."

"Well, I'm really sorry about New Year's."

"It's okay. If you want, there's a box of Valentine cookies. You're welcome to them." She pointed to the small box on the countertop.

"Thanks. I better be going. Thanks for the cookies." He walked out and she smiled at his back, happy that he was getting help.

When Josie came back into the kitchen half an hour later, she looked like she was on cloud nine. She danced around and even took hold of Sara's hands and twirled around the room.

"What's gotten into you?" Sara stopped her from spinning again.

"Larry. Larry Hamill. I'm in love with Larry Hamill!" She screamed.

"Really?" Sara laughed. "So quickly?"

"Sure. If you can fall for Allen fast, why can't I fall for Larry faster?" Her friend frowned, and Sara laughed. "He's caring, funny, smart, and so very romantic. What did you think would happen with me and a guy like that?"

"I don't know. I've known Larry my whole life. I guess I've never thought of him that way."

"Good." Her friend squinted her eyes at her and gave her a look, trying to scare her. "You've got your own man. Leave mine alone."

Sara laughed. "I promise. I will never fall in love with your Larry Hamill."

Josie smiled. "Good, then I guess we can remain best friends." Sara laughed and hugged her best friend.

At lunchtime, her mother stopped in. She was dressed up and looked wonderful. It was the first time in a long time that she'd seen her mother wearing a dress and lipstick; she was shocked.

"Where are you off to?" She smiled and hugged her. "You look wonderful."

"Oh, well, thank you, dear." Her mother messed with her hair a little. "I'm just meeting an old friend for lunch."

"Really?" Sara leaned back against the counter and smiled. "Do I know this person?"

"Yes, well, Eugene Leachman has been a family friend for years."

Sara coughed. "Doctor Leachman?" When her mother nodded, she smiled. "You bagged a doctor."

Her mother shook her head. "Really, where did you learn such language?" Her mother smiled.

Just then Becca walked in from the front room, smiling. "Did you hear that mom bagged a doctor?" Sara looked at her mother and they broke out laughing.

EPILOGUE

The Sunday after Valentine's Day, the sun was shining and there wasn't a cloud in the sky. Allen leaned back against the large driftwood and smiled at Sara and Beast playing in the surf. He knew the water was probably very cold, but they splashed around like neither of them cared.

The large picnic blanket and empty plates around him would have to be packed up soon, judging by the level of the sun, but for now, he smiled and laughed at his two greatest loves playing in the water.

Mr. Mathis had been released when his wife had confessed to stalking Sara. Allen had been told by Robert that the woman was being evaluated at the local hospital for mental stability. Apparently, she'd been posing as a prospective home buyer in Pride. She'd been going around town telling everyone she was moving in soon.

Watching the pair play in the water, her hair flowing wild in the wind, he remembered what she'd looked like last night wearing the sexy lace she'd surprised him with.

He'd been shocked and pleased and had enjoyed taking his time slowly peeling it off her.

How had he gotten so lucky? Sara laughed, and he looked over. Here he was on the perfect beach, with the dog, and the woman of his dream from so long ago. Just then Beast rushed up to him and stood and shook himself clean of the water. Beads of water smelling like wet dog rained down on him and the blanket.

"Beast!" He jumped up and tried to escape the attack. Sara laughed from her position by the water.

"He just wants you to join in the fun." She smiled and tossed a stick into the water. Beast bolted after it.

Allen walked over and grabbed Sara around the waist, spinning her around. "What do you say we head home and have a different kind of fun?" He leaned over and kissed her until both their heads were spinning.

"Mmm, sounds like a great plan." She started walking backward, but he stopped her.

"This is going to last, you and I." She stopped and looked up at him.

"Of course, it is." She smiled, holding his hand.

"Good. I don't want it to ever end." He pulled her closer.

"Never." She smiled up at him.

"Good, then you won't have any objections when we get married."

"Of course not." She smiled at him, looking pleased.

"Good. Just so you know, that's where this is heading."

"That's good. Because I was starting to figure out how to bake another cake for you."

"Oh, no. What would this one look like?"

She smiled and stood back from him, her arms crossed

over her chest, her head tilted to the side as if thinking. "One with you down on one knee, a diamond ring in your hands."

He laughed. "Like this one?" He pulled a small box out of his pocket. His sister had brought him his grandmother's ring last month. He'd brought it along today knowing the time was right. That Sara was the right person.

She looked stunned, much to his enjoyment.

"Well?" He nodded towards the box. "Don't you want to see it?"

She took the small box from his hands. Her fingers shook as she flipped the lid open.

"It was my grandmother's, so it's a little old-fashioned."

"It's perfect." She looked up at him quickly. "It's perfect," she repeated.

"Good." He smiled as he removed the ring and waited for her to hold out her fingers, so he could slip it onto her ring finger. He dropped down on his knee. Beast came running over, thinking it was a new game. After several attempts to push him away, Sara said,

"Sit." Beast sat and looked up at her.

"Perfect. Now you can both propose." She smiled and nodded. "Continue."

He laughed.

"Sara, would you do me...um...us, the honor of marrying me...um, us?" He slid the ring on her finger.

"Yes!" She smiled and pulled his hand until they were spinning as the dog ran circles around them.

PROLOGUE

*K*atie Derby sat across from Jason and wondered why she had agreed to meet him at the coffee shop. She'd been embarrassed since Lynda's party several weeks ago when she'd gotten drunk and admitted to him all the years she'd had secret feelings for him. Then she had topped it off with a stupid kiss. One that he had held still through, very still. It had been apparent to her that he didn't feel the same way about her. Now she sat fidgeting with her napkin in her lap, wishing to be anywhere else on the planet.

"It's not that… Well, it's just that… I had never…" He was mumbling, and she could tell he was terrified. His beautiful blue eyes were searching her face.

"Jason," she interrupted him, trying to explain before he said something that would rip her heart out, "I don't want you to think – well, I was very drunk. It was just a mistake. I don't want there to be any weirdness between us." A little part of her heart broke off and floated to the floor when he looked almost relieved.

Before he could respond, her cell phone rang. Seeing her brother's number, she hit ignore. Not two seconds later, she saw her father's number and she hit ignore again.

Looking back at Jason, she noticed the fear in his eyes and could already tell the weirdness between them had settled in. She took a deep breath but wanted to pound her head on the table.

"Katie, I don't know..." Her phone rang for the third time. Looking down she saw her mother's number.

"I'm sorry, Jason, I better..." she nodded to her phone.

"Sure." He looked like he wanted to bolt for the door.

"Hello, Mom, what's so important?" she answered, stepping away from the table and walking towards the back of the almost empty coffee shop.

"Katie, oh thank God you answered. I wanted to talk to you before you heard a bunch of lies from anyone else."

Her mother cleared her throat and then continued on. "Well, sweetie, first of all, I wanted to tell you something, because I know it's going to come out very soon, and I thought you would want to hear the truth instead of the lies that are going around on the news, or hearing something completely false from the police."

Katie waited, knowing that she wouldn't be able to interrupt her mother once she had started.

"Twenty-six years ago, after your father and I had a huge falling out, I went to Italy to recover from the pain your father had caused, and ... well... I had an affair with a man named Damiano Cardone. We had a son. I left them in Italy to come back and divorce your father, but he... well, we didn't get a divorce. Anyway, I kept in touch with them, and in a roundabout way, Damiano and I are married. Well, that's not the important part. Four years later I visited them and when I returned back home, I realized I was pregnant again and … well… this time I had you. Obviously, it was too late to keep it from your father since he had already found out I was pregnant. He was just so happy about it."

Katie felt herself starting to hyperventilate.

"I just couldn't break your father's heart, so I made him believe you were his. Damiano Cardone is your biological father, honey, not Rodrick. I'm sorry I had to tell you over the…" Katie dropped her phone. Her ears were ringing, and her vision grayed around the edges. Jason was beside her, yelling at her to breathe. The last thing she saw before she passed out was Jason's blue eyes, hovering over her.

SECRET SEDUCTION

CHAPTER 1

atie sat on the soft sand on the beach and thought about her life as the sun was setting. A strong and independent woman, she thought she knew what she wanted out of life. But then last year her mother had thrown a wrench into her carefully laid out plans. It had been a year since she'd seen or talked to anyone from her past life. The only thing that she still wanted, and had always wanted, was Jason.

Jason Keaton had been her best friend, and for one wonderful year, her roommate. He was the only man Katie had ever wanted to be with.

Now as she watched the sun setting over the water, she knew she had been naive. She had spent years of her life trusting people, only to find out that they had all been using her. Her friends had quickly turned on her, her mother had lied to her, Jason had even... well, that was more complicated. She didn't want to think about Jason. She'd tried and tried not to think about him for the last year.

Now she was sitting on a beautiful beach in a foreign country watching the bright colors of the sunset, and all she had to her name was the small backpack of clothes on her back. No apartment, no furniture, no friends, no one to tie her down.

She'd been to more places than she could count since leaving the states, from Pairs to Madrid, and Berlin to Athens. She had spent the last year crisscrossing Europe and enjoying every minute of her venture.

The next day she had plans to meet her biological father, Damiano Cardone, for the first time. She didn't know who to trust anymore, so she had kept to herself since her mother's big reveal.

She didn't know if she would keep her meeting with her real father, or as she liked to call him, her biological daddy, or BD for short. The meeting was scheduled for the next day in his Athens office building. He owned one of Europe's largest businesses, New Edges. There were even branches of the business in the US run by his son, her biological brother Dante. Katie didn't quite know what the company did. Export, she thought, but she knew he was as powerful as the man who'd raised her was.

Rodrick Derby, the man she still thought of as her real dad (RD for short) had been just as deceived as she had. Believing his wife had been faithful to him for almost thirty years, he had raised Katie, not knowing the secrets his wife had been keeping.

Turning her thoughts to the other man who'd been lied to for years, she thought of what she could possibly say to Damiano. What could he say to her? They had both been robbed. Robbed of time and knowledge of each other's existence by a woman she no longer wanted to call her own flesh and blood.

Just then she heard a noise and quickly looked over her shoulder. The beach had grown darker and she couldn't see anything or anyone around her. The quiet beach was deserted. She could hear the surf hit the soft sand and enjoyed the mellow rhythm. She sat near the edge of the tall grass and looked to where the noise had come from, behind her, near the tree line. She realized this part of the beach was too far off the pathway for it to be another tourist. It might have been a local, or a deer or some other kind of animal.

She realized she was sitting alone in the dark, so she quickly stood up, dusted the sand from her jeans, and picked up her backpack. She started to walk back towards civilization and a row of hotels that she knew where just inside town. The tall buildings were lined up along the horseshoe-shaped beach and were no doubt full of tourists. Instead of stopping and getting a room when she'd gotten into town, she'd walked by them, straight to the beach, which had called to her. She'd walked right by all the happy families and couples enjoying the warm water and hot sun on the beach until she'd felt satisfied she'd worked out a few things in her mind. She'd ended up on the deserted part of the beach, alone.

She was desperately trying to find some answers to who she was, what she now wanted out of life. It had taken just over a year for her to contact Damiano. He was her biological father, and she was curious to meet the man.

When she had contacted him, Katie had been insistent that she didn't want her mother, Kathleen, there when she met him, so they had arranged a meeting at his Athens office. Damiano's voice had been strong, deep, and rich, and even with his accent, his words were easily discernible. He sounded eager for the meeting and she could tell he was just as nervous as she was.

She'd traveled to Athens via train and bus in under a week. But when she'd arrived, she had continued southwest until she'd hit the coastal town of Alimos. It was just a quick twenty-minute drive to Athens and Damiano's office, but she felt a little more level-headed staying outside the larger city, in a smaller, more secluded area.

Walking out of the tall grass area, she hit the soft, smooth sand and heard a twig snap right behind her. When she turned around to look, there was nobody around. Turning and picking up her pace a little more, she tried to keep her mind occupied by remembering the multiple day train ride south she'd taken. It had been a very nervous trip for her.

When she had left Denmark, her heart was light, her pulse pounding with adrenaline and excitement. She couldn't wipe the eager look off her face. A few days later, by the time she'd reached Greece, her feelings of excitement had been replaced with nervous dread. Her palms were sweaty, her face flushed, and she couldn't sit still in her seat. The beautiful scenery that passed her by in the train's large windows just didn't hold her interest anymore. She would sit and stare out at it, unseeing. Instead, visions of the meeting to come flashed before her eyes. What would he look like? Did she look like him? Would he be kind? How would she greet him? Should she give him a hug? Would he cry?

Several times, she had felt like everyone on the train had been watching her. After all, her face had been on every news channel last year in America. She'd had a hard time going anywhere without people pointing at her. When she'd gone to classes, the kids would make fun of her. Even at the grocery store, people in line would see her face on the tabloids and then look at her. Sometimes she would see a mix of pity and amusement in their faces. It wasn't as if she'd asked for all the attention, unlike some of the other women she'd seen on those same tabloids. She'd been thrust into overnight stardom thanks to her mother's infidelity and her family name.

Being the daughter of Rodrick Derby, the second of the prominent New England Derby's, was big news on its own. But when it turned out that she was actually the daughter of Damiano Cardone, entrepreneur of New Edges, a multimillion dollar company, she became even bigger news.

On the train trip there, she'd thought about getting off and heading someplace else. But she had never chickened out before in life and wasn't about to start now, so she had continued on her path. She didn't consider leaving the US as running away; instead, she chose to think of it as a necessary break.

She looked back down the beach to where she'd just come from, trying to see if someone or something was following her. She couldn't see anything except the water reflecting off the dark sky. Since it was a new moon, the clear sky was filled just with stars which, although bright, were not bright enough to light up the dark beach. It was too dark to see if there was anyone around. She felt the cool breeze hit her face and smelled the salt water and sand in the air. Although it was warm, she felt a shiver travel up her spine. She pulled her jacket closed and tried to keep her eyes and mind focused on the bright lights ahead of her.

Maybe there was a journalist following her? After all, the media had been almost unbearable back in the States; she'd been followed, photographed, and questioned every time she'd left her small dorm room back in Boston. They had exploited every detail of her life, including her friends, her party habits, and even the classes she was taking. They especially focused on the fact that she'd been going to school there for five years with no real end in sight. She had felt like her whole life was under a microscope.

The betrayal of her close friends had been immediate. For weeks after, they could be seen on every news station telling her life story and every detail of their friendship to anyone who would pay them enough. Even Brenda, her very best friend since second grade, had been seen on TMZ, exposing Katie's party habits. She had even told them that Katie didn't know what she wanted to do with her life. But it had taken seeing Jason's face on the television to make her pack a small bag and buy a one-way ticket to Europe.

That night, she had watched as he exited his car outside his dorm room, his dark sandy hair looking like he'd just run his hands through it. He hadn't shaved that morning, which always gave him a rough, boyish look Katie loved. He had been walking to the door when a swarm of reporters started yelling questions at him.

"How long have you and Katie Derby been seeing each other?" one shouted.

"When are you and Katie getting married?" another one could be heard.

"What is your relationship with Katie Derby?"

She could tell that the questions had taken him by surprise. Instead of keeping his head down, he looked into the camera. It seemed to take forever for him to start answering. Katie had gotten so upset when she heard his reply.

He had looked so dumb-founded, his blue eyes searching the crowd like he didn't know what was happening.

"Katie and I are just fr…"

He stuttered, almost as if it had taken all his conscious thought to try and figure out their relationship. She knew what they were, she could easily shout it from every rooftop. How hard could it be to say it to a bunch of strangers? They were best friends.

She'd been hurt, so hurt, that when she had slammed off the television, interrupting his statement, she had pushed the button so hard that it had caused the small set to fall off the stand. The set had wobbled at first and she thought about trying to catch it, but then she watched as it fell forward and landed hard, shattering the display in a million pieces. Glass and plastic had fallen all over her black-and-white polka dot rug, and she realized she didn't care.

Several girls stopped in the hallway and looked at her, then continued on their way, giggling, and no doubt talking about her.

That was the last time she had seen anyone she knew -- her friends, her family. She hadn't even officially dropped out of school.

She packed her small backpack, leaving everything behind: her new iPhone, her laptop, her designer clothes and shoes, everything. She took a cab to the airport and booked the next flight out, which just happened to be to Paris.

She had spent the last year of her life traveling around Europe, spending her savings, not once touching the credit cards from her old life.

She'd seen places she had always wanted to visit. Even though she kept to the smaller towns, the cheaper hotels, and the inexpensive restaurants, she had still been enjoying herself. And the main thing was, she'd kept her mind off her problems, at least when she'd kept busy.

Every time she had had some downtime over the last year, she had always reverted back to thinking about the betrayal, about her mother, her friends, and most importantly, Jason. She tried not to think about her problems too often. She wasn't really wallowing in pity, more like taking a break from reality.

Looking around her, she felt a little relieved that she'd hit the main pathway back into town. Here the wood planks of the walkway creaked under her feet. She could barely see the path leading to the lights and safety of the small city and couldn't even see her own feet in front of her, causing her to stumble a few times on uneven planks jutting out from the path. She thought she heard a board creak behind her and turned quickly to look. Seeing nothing, she quickened her pace. Was someone following her? She felt like she was being toyed with. In all her time being alone in Europe, she'd never felt threatened or scared. Now, however, she would have done anything to have a friend with her.

She could feel her fear vibrating throughout her entire body. Her hands shook as she held onto her backpack, and her breath was coming in quick bursts. She felt like running but didn't want to seem like one of those crazy women who went running and screaming because of a small noise.

When she reached the clearing of the first street and could finally see her own feet in the light, she started to relax and released a large sigh of relief. She had no time to scream as a black bag was tossed over her head, and she was grabbed by several large hands.

This is a work of fiction. Names, characters, places, and incidents either are the product of the author's imagination or are used fictitiously, and any resemblance to actual persons, living or dead, business establishments, events or locales is entirely coincidental.

MY SWEET VALENTINE

DIGITAL ISBN: 978-1-942896-27-2

PRINT ISBN: 978-1-496166-22-7

Copyright © 2014 Jill Sanders

All rights reserved.

Copyeditor: Erica Ellis – inkdeepediting.com

Missy's Moment

Breaking Travis

Roping Ryan

Wild Bride

Corey's Catch

Tessa's Turn

The Grayton Series

Last Resort

Someday Beach

Rip Current

In Too Deep

Swept Away

High Tide

Lucky Series

Unlucky In Love

Sweet Resolve

Best of Luck

A Little Luck

Silver Cove Series

Silver Lining

French Kiss

Happy Accident

Hidden Charm

A Silver Cove Christmas

Entangled Series – Paranormal Romance

The Awakening

The Beckoning

The Ascension

Haven, Montana Series

Closer to You

Never Let Go

Holding On

Pride Oregon Series

A Dash of Love

My Kind of Love

Season of Love

Tis the Season

Dare to Love

Where I Belong

Wildflowers Series

Summer Nights

Summer Heat

Stand Alone Books

Twisted Rock

For a complete list of books:

http://JillSanders.com

ABOUT THE AUTHOR

Jill Sanders is a New York Times, USA Today, and international bestselling author of Sweet Contemporary Romance, Romantic Suspense, Western Romance, and Paranormal Romance novels. With over 55 books in eleven series, translations into several different languages, and audiobooks there's plenty to choose from. Look for Jill's bestselling stories wherever romance books are sold or visit her at jillsanders.com

Jill comes from a large family with six siblings, including an identical twin. She was raised in the Pacific Northwest and later relocated to Colorado for college and a successful IT career before discovering her talent for writing sweet and sexy page-turners. After Colorado, she decided to move south, living in Texas and now making her home along the Emerald Coast of Florida. You will find that the settings of several of her series are inspired by her time spent living in these areas. She has two sons and off-set the testosterone in her house by adopting three furry little ladies that provide her company while she's locked in her writing cave. She enjoys heading to the beach, hiking, swimming, wine-tasting, and pickleball with her husband, and of course writing. If you have read any of her books, you may also notice that there is a love of food, especially sweets! She has been blamed for a few added pounds by her assistant, editor, and fans... donuts or pie anyone?

facebook.com/JillSandersBooks

twitter.com/JillMSanders

bookbub.com/authors/jill-sanders

CPSIA information can be obtained
at www.ICGtesting.com
Printed in the USA
LVHW020008160721
692785LV00012B/1183